SPECIAL MESSAGE TO READERS

HOUSE OF FOOLS

Toby Stewart has been invited by her sister Anne to visit her at Fool's End, the manor where she works as a personal secretary to a famous author, and after his recent death has stayed on to catalogue his papers and manuscripts. But on arriving, Toby is dismayed to learn that Anne has mysteriously disappeared — without taking any of her possessions and without informing her employers. And most everyone there, it seems, has something to hide. Did Anne leave of her own volition — or has she perhaps been murdered . . . ?

Books by V. J. Banis
in the Linford Mystery Library:

THE WOLVES OF CRAYWOOD
THE GLASS PAINTING
WHITE JADE
DARKWATER
I AM ISABELLA
THE GLASS HOUSE
MOON GARDEN
THE SECOND HOUSE
ROSE POINT
THE DEVIL'S DANCE
SHADOWS

V. J. BANIS

HOUSE OF FOOLS

Complete and Unabridged

LINFORD
Leicester

First published in Great Britain

First Linford Edition
published 2015

A catalogue record for this book is available
from the British Library.

ISBN 978–1–4448–2446–9

Published by
F. A. Thorpe (Publishing)
Anstey, Leicestershire

Set by Words & Graphics Ltd.
Anstey, Leicestershire
Printed and bound in Great Britain by
T. J. International Ltd., Padstow, Cornwall

This book is printed on acid-free paper

118978117

1

Fool's End was lovely at first view, even if one knew of those dizzying cliffs beyond, that spilled recklessly down to a lashing ocean. The massive house looked cool and reposed, silhouetted against the gray March sky. It looked inviting too, in a harsh way, even if one felt less and less like a daring adventurer and more and more like a foolish young woman of two-and-twenty.

I set my father's suitcase down, partly to postpone my arrival, and partly from sheer necessity. My shoulder ached and I was out of breath. Although the distance was probably less than a mile, I felt as though I had walked forever since the wobbly little bus had set me down at the road below.

The vast windows of that house seemed to stare down at me, and at once my imagination peopled each one with watching and curious strangers.

Curious they might well be. I did not know if Anne had told her employers that her younger sister might be arriving. I thought I remembered that she had and that it was all right; but that might only have been wishful thinking on my part. At any rate, even if she had told them, they wouldn't be expecting me now. Anne and I had talked tentatively of my coming in mid-April. Now that I was here, a month early to surprise my sister, I was increasingly conscious of how tentative those plans had been.

I tried to see myself as those watching windows saw me: a silly-looking woman seated none too decorously on the end of her suitcase, which was unmistakably a man's case — old, and not a very elegant one at that.

Silly. Yes, that was how Anne had described me. I did have blonde hair, which was supposed to help, but did none of those wonderful things blonde hair was supposed to do; hair that refused to shimmer or cascade or curl charmingly, as it did for those handsome creatures one saw in television commercials; hair that

2

did nothing but fall straight down from my head in long yellow sheets. And what else but 'silly' would apply to a woman who had one gray eye and one green one?

I sighed, wishing that the sense of adventure and excitement had lasted a little longer — until I was inside, at least. Sometimes it didn't do to think of the practical aspects of a situation. Now that I was here it did no good telling myself I probably shouldn't have come. I was here, and short of fleeing back down the hill, which would look sillier still to any watchers, there was nothing I could do but continue up. I lifted the suitcase again and started toward the house.

One of those many windows truly was watching me. It winked its curtain at me as I drew near. It was too quick for me to tell who had held that curtain aside to watch me, but the discovery added to my nervousness. By the time I reached the great carved door and summoned the courage to bang the heavy brass knocker, I had called myself every kind of fool there was.

I hoped in silent desperation that it

would be Anne who opened the door. Dear Anne, who seemed always to be getting me out of some scrape or other. I would let her explain my presence here to her employers and, though she would scold me for my impetuosity, she would manage to see that things came out all right in the end.

However, it was not Anne who answered my knock. The woman who greeted me was tall and handsome, elegant in a gaunt sort of way. Although she was womanly there was a tempered steel firmness about her that contradicted her femininity. Her hair was silvery, so completely so that I guessed she had hastened the natural process.

From the description Anne had given me in her letters I guessed that this was Barbara Christian. Anne had said she was formidable. Even at first glance, I was quite willing to agree.

'Is Miss Stewart in?' I asked, instinctively clinging to my hope that Anne would take over the task of making explanations.

'Miss Stewart?'

4

'Miss Anne Stewart. I'm her sister Toby.'

'I see,' she said. But Mrs. Christian's expression said that she did not see at all. She looked quite perplexed. I tried to think what I ought to say to make things clearer. For a long moment we stood on opposite sides of the threshold, staring at one another in some confusion. Finally she made some sort of decision and swung the door wider, saying, 'Perhaps you had better come in.'

I came in as quickly as the heavy bag would permit, not wanting her to change her mind. My impression of Mrs. Christian was that she would be quite capable of closing the door on me and leaving me standing out there until I went away.

'Come in here, please,' she said, indicating a door off the vast entry hall. She had a grating manner, imperious and aloof; but I reminded myself that she was in effect the lady of this house now and I was only the relative of an employee.

'Certainly,' I said, following her into a rather gloomy front room. There were two men there, one of them seated and one of them standing by the mantle, both watching the door with what seemed to me an air of tense expectancy. I was of course the center of all attention as I came in. I could not have felt more foolish.

'This,' Mrs. Christian said, as though it were an announcement of grave importance, 'is Miss Stewart's sister.'

The man who was seated dropped a glass of wine he was holding. It crashed loudly on the stone hearth. No one seemed to mind; they were much too absorbed in staring at me. I had an awful realization that Anne had not mentioned me at all, or my proposed visit.

I stood there dumbly looking back at them until one of the men, the one standing by the mantle, came toward me with a smile.

'You're Toby, of course,' he said, taking my hand in his. 'I should have known when I saw you coming up the drive. You look exactly as Anne described you.'

'Then she did mention me?' I asked with a slight sense of relief.

'She talked of you often,' he said. 'I'm William Christian. This is my stepmother, Mrs. Christian.' He paused before adding, I thought a trifle reluctantly, 'And my stepbrother, Grant Christian.'

All I could think to say was, 'How do you do.' Anne had told me that both of the Christian men were good-looking. In Grant's case that was certainly true. He was slim and handsome and had inherited his mother's dry elegance.

But to call William Christian goodlooking was to grossly understate the case. I thought at once that I had never seen so handsome a man. He was not small like Grant, but incredibly tall and powerfully built, but without any unseemly bulk. He had dark hair and enough irregularity of feature to keep that handsome face from cloying. He made one think of gambling casinos and racing cars and very dry martinis — none of which I was in the least familiar with. I was completely taken by him.

That might have contributed to the faint gleam of amusement I saw in his eyes. I had a sudden suspicion that

William Christian understood my predicament. Worse, if I was any judge, he was enjoying it.

At any rate, I did not understand it, not all of it. There was no sign of Anne and no one had made any move to summon her. Apparently I was expected to supply an explanation first. I looked away from William Christian's gleaming eyes and spoke to his stepmother.

'I've come to visit my sister. I wonder if I could see her?'

They exchanged glances. It was plain that they were deciding silently who should give me some piece of information, but what information? An idea came to me suddenly and I looked anxiously at William Christian again. 'You spoke of my sister just now in the past tense,' I said. 'Surely you don't mean . . . ?'

'Don't be alarmed,' he said quickly. 'It's nothing like that. But your sister isn't here any longer.'

'I don't understand.'

'She left Fool's End two days ago,' Barbara explained.

I was completely flabbergasted. 'You

mean she resigned her job here?'

Barbara smiled drily. 'Not exactly,' she said. 'The truth is, she just left, without any sort of explanation. We were as astonished as you.'

I couldn't think what to make of it, what to say. Nothing under the sun could have surprised me more. It was so unlike Anne — dear, practical, organized, plan-ahead Anne. 'What forwarding address did she leave?' I asked.

'None.'

I must have looked as if I was going to fall over, because William put a hand on my arm to steady me. 'Easy,' he said. 'You'd better sit down.' He led me to a big overstuffed chair. I sat in it gratefully, but I couldn't say anything for several moments.

'Was your sister expecting you?' he asked in a gentle voice.

'Yes. No. Well . . . ' I shook my head and managed a faint smile. 'I suppose I ought to explain. Anne expected her work to be finished next month. I was going to meet her here and then we planned to go on to San Francisco and put down roots there. We lost our parents a year ago, you see, and home has been rather sad for us. So while Anne was here, I've been selling things and putting things in storage and what have you.'

I looked up to find them all watching me closely. They had every reason to, but still it made me uncomfortable and I looked down at my hands in my lap. 'As it happens, I finished early,' I went on. 'I found a couple who wanted virtually everything and I sold it to them and finished things up sooner than I expected. I meant to surprise Anne by coming here a month early. I thought I could find a place nearby and wait for her to finish.'

The last part wasn't the truth. In my foolishness I had been certain that the Christians would let me stay here and that there would be enough work for me to do to earn my keep. Now, however, I didn't want to admit to them how presumptuous I had been.

My explanation was greeted by a long silence. It was Grant, who had said nothing until now, who broke it. 'It looks as though I need a fresh glass. Will you

10

have some sherry, Miss Stewart?'

'Yes, thank you,' I said gratefully. I had never had anything alcoholic to drink before. He brought a small glass of a tawny liquid. I took a taste of it and found that it had a pleasant nut-like flavor. I suppose it was only my imagination, but it seemed to ease my consternation a little.

'Oh,' I exclaimed suddenly. As my thoughts cleared, memory came back to me. 'I'm afraid I've completely forgotten my manners. I meant to express my sympathy for your loss. I suppose it sounds effusive but when Anne wrote me of Walter McKay's death, I felt that a literary tradition had ended.'

Barbara acknowledged my remarks with a smile that seemed to me oddly condescending. 'Thank you,' she said, 'although I'm afraid the literary tradition ended some years ago. Your sister had little to do as his secretary, mostly busy work I'm afraid, to keep him occupied. The truth is she's had more work since my brother's death, helping us with the estate, than she had before.'

'It was kind of you to keep her on as you did,' I said.

'Not at all; she was most helpful.' She did not add, although one read it into her comment, that Anne had been ungrateful to leave as she did.

'Did Anne offer an explanation as to why she was going?' I asked, looking from one to the other of them. William had been quiet since leading me to the chair, but I saw now that he watched me with anything but a casual look. I felt that he was weighing what I had said, looking for something, but I could not tell what.

'I was wondering if you could tell us that,' he said. 'Did she offer any comments in her letters?'

'No, only . . . ' I frowned thoughtfully, remembering. 'There was something, but I don't know what exactly. She told me in her last letter that she had learned something, something very exciting, but she said she couldn't tell me about it yet. All she would give me was a clue, one word to tease me. She liked to do that — tease me, I mean.'

'What was the word?' William asked.

'Diamonds,' I said.

My explanations of my appearance had dissipated that tension that had filled the room when I entered; but now, suddenly, it was back fourfold. Barbara's sharp intake of breath was clearly audible and Grant looked as though he might lose another glass of sherry. Only William appeared to be calm, but I dropped my gaze in time to see him clenching and unclenching his fists tensely.

'Intriguing,' he said aloud, smiling as though the atmosphere had not changed at all. 'But not very helpful, I'm afraid. The only diamonds in my possession are in a set of cufflinks which I saw in my jewelry box earlier today. And no one else has mentioned any missing stones.'

'You're sure there was nothing more?' Grant asked. 'Nothing in her letters that could be a clue?'

'For instance?' I asked, genuinely ignorant of any such clues in Anne's letters.

'Could your sister have become engaged?' Barbara offered.

'I think she would have told me that,' I answered.

'But mightn't she have meant to surprise you, as you planned to surprise her? Diamonds do mean engagement to a girl, and an elopement might explain her abrupt departure. And as you have said yourself, she had no reason to expect you for another month. Probably by then she planned on being with you and telling you about it in person.'

'Perhaps,' I said reluctantly. Privately I was unconvinced. Anne was not the sort to elope. As for falling in love, she was no doubt as susceptible to that as any other woman, but I was certain that had it occurred I would have heard about it from the very beginning, every detail. Anne had never kept secrets.

I kept these thoughts to myself, though, without fully knowing why I did so. I had an unaccountable feeling that the explanation was too pat, and had been seized upon too quickly by the Christians. I still could not understand Anne's leaving, and nothing that had been said had made that any more understandable.

'I've been thinking,' William said, speaking slowly as if an idea were just forming itself in his mind. 'As my stepmother said, there's been more work since her brother's death than there was before. There still is, and I think we could use some help with it. Perhaps you would want to stay on for a few days and take your sister's place.'

'Oh, I hadn't even thought of that,' I said, caught off guard by the suggestion. 'But there doesn't seem to be much point in it now, does there? I mean, my only purpose in coming was to be with my sister, and if she's not here . . .'

'You said yourself you've nothing to go back for, or to,' he said. 'And anyway, if you leave here your sister will never know how to track you down. Once she's gone home and found that you've come here, she'll surely get in touch immediately. You ought to wait here at least until you've heard from her, don't you think?'

I thought that, on the slimmest of evidence, the Christian family seemed quite convinced that Anne was going home, but looking up into William's manly face I had an impression that it would be very difficult to refuse him anything once he had put his mind to it.

'But what could she do?' Barbara asked. 'Do you type, Miss Stewart, or take dictation?'

I shook my head. 'I'm afraid I have very little training or experience. My experience is limited to baby-sitting and domestic work . . . and working for a summer in a gift shop back home.'

'She could look after Jamie,' William said. 'He really needs someone to keep an eye on him.'

I had completely forgotten until now that there was another member of the family whom I had not yet met. Jamie McKay was Walter McKay's orphaned grandson. If I remembered Anne's letters correctly, he would be nine years old, or close thereto. His parents, Walter McKay's son and daughter-in-law, had died in an accident a year before, leaving the boy with his ailing grandfather and the Christians. Anne had spoken of him often in her letters and had been quite fond of him.

They seemed to be waiting for some comment from me. I tried to examine my thoughts and feelings. William Christian had made some reasonable statements. I had no place to go, and it would be easier for Anne to find me here than if I went on to San Francisco. If, I thought swiftly, she really were looking for me. That was the reason for my indecision. I was more than puzzled by my sister's mysterious disappearance; I was vaguely frightened by it as well. There were undercurrents of feelings and innuendoes moving through this room between these people.

'I don't know what to say,' I admitted aloud. 'Or how to decide.'

'Well then,' William said, 'don't decide anything, not tonight at least. It's getting late. It will be night soon and you've had a long trip. The least we can do is invite — no, insist — that you stay the night. In the morning you can go or stay, as you think best.'

'But I don't want to impose,' I said. That was not quite the truth either. I was tired and his suggestion made sense. Probably I was letting my imagination

17

run away with me because I was tired. In the morning perhaps things would seem much clearer to me.

'Nonsense,' Grant Christian sided with his stepbrother. 'It's the least we can do when you've had such a shock. Don't you agree, Mother?'

'But of course,' she said smoothly. I had to suppress a shudder; her tone gave the lie to her words. 'Suppose I take you up to a room and you can get yourself refreshed. Mrs. Haskins will be serving dinner before too long.'

'All right,' I agreed wearily. I excused myself to my hosts and went with Mrs. Christian into the hall.

'I'll have the houseman bring your bag up,' she said, leading the way up the wide and curving stairs. They were unlighted at this time of day, but the windows were high and narrow, allowing very little light to come through. I had to hold the banister firmly and watch each step to avoid tripping.

'I wonder if I could ask one favor,' I said, moving as quickly as I could after my hostess, who seemed to have no

18

difficulty with the dim lighting. 'Would it be convenient to let me have my sister's room?'

I thought, without being certain, that she hesitated for a fraction of a second. 'Surely,' she said, without looking back. 'It will be no trouble at all.'

The room into which she ushered me was on the second of three floors, to the front of the house. There was a large canopied bed against one wall, but the impression was that it had been added to what was originally a sitting room. The furnishings were bright and colorful, and surprisingly cheerful after the gloom of the halls and the parlor downstairs. I went to the window and pulled back the chintz curtains to peer out. It gave a wide view of the drive that curved up from the road below, and the front lawns. I remembered being watched from one of the windows as I approached the house. William Christian had admitted watching me. Had it been from this same window? I wondered.

'This was your sister's room,' Barbara said behind me. 'I think you'll find it quite comfortable. There's a connecting bath there, but the other bedroom is unoccupied, so you'll have the bath to yourself.'

She started from the room, adding, 'I'll have your things brought up. We generally eat at six.'

I thanked her again for her hospitality, and managed to smile brightly until the door was closed after her. Then I stopped smiling. I thought about Anne, and about her first letters from Fool's End, letters in which she had mentioned again and again the view from her room — a view of ocean waters crashing against rocks.

'Sometimes I wake in the night,' she wrote, 'and hear the waves like angry beasts trying to reach my snug little room. I curl up under the blanket on my trim little studio bed and listen for hours to the sounds of the sea.'

Barbara Christian had lied to me about this room; it was not Anne's room. The question which now lingered in my mind was, if she had lied about this one point, might she not have lied about others as well?

20

Close on the heels of that question was another. Why had she found it necessary to lie at all? People lied to conceal the truth. What truth were these people trying to conceal from me?

2

The house was named for the fool's end of land on which it sat, a dead-end street of a promontory that went nowhere but jutted raggedly into the ocean like a gnarled and solemn finger. To what did it point? I wondered. Where would it send me?

Fool's End, as everyone who read must know, was the home of Walter McKay. It was in this retreat that he had penned those masterpieces — the novels, the plays, the essays — that had brought him the acclaim, the respect, and finally the awe of the world. 'He was,' one of my teachers had said of him, 'the perfect writer.' His was a gift, however, that needed no instructor to assure you of its perfection. He wrote of and to all men, of universal truths and universal fears and universal loves.

How excited we had been, Anne and I, when the job for which she had applied turned out to be that of secretary to Walter McKay. He had not written in twenty years, although in that interval there had been published two volumes of his work — one a collection of his personal letters that brought to life many of the greats of the past fifty years, but none so vividly as McKay himself; the other a rambling assortment of notes from his journals that had since their publication produced a hundred imitators but not, alas, one McKay.

Then had come the great shock of his death. So quietly had he lived these last twenty years, that much of the world seemed already to believe him dead. I heard the news from the television.

Anne's letter did not come until a week later. It was full of those heart-breaking glimpses into the last hours. In the months of working for him Anne had not lost her reverence for this literary giant; but she had, I knew from her letters, grown equally fond of him as a person, an individual. It was strange that of a man whom much of the world loved and revered, she should write:

23

'He lived in what he considered a loveless world. As a young man, a restless gypsy, he lived apart from his own family. When he met his wife he loved her completely and with all of his heart. When she died he realized that he ought to have given some of his love to others, but it was too late; they had long since come to look upon him as one of those relations one cannot like but cannot afford to dislike. There is only his grandson, little Jamie, now nine years old. They are fond of one another, grandfather and grandson, but there is a chasm of more than sixty years between them which cannot often be bridged.'

I knew how pleased Anne was when the heirs had asked her to stay on until affairs were settled. It was not only the question of a job; she could have found another. In time she would have to find another anyway, but she had wanted to linger over those papers and bits of miscellany that were his legacy.

Was I to believe that she had suddenly run away from that legacy because she had fallen in love?

My things were brought up soon afterward by a lumbering brute of a man who spoke only in grunted syllables. I suppose my imagination was by now working overtime, as it was wont to do, but he made me uneasy. His surliness was as tangible as the dirty shirt he wore, and too deep-set to be the result of a single specific cause. This was a man who simply disliked the world and its inhabitants. If one found that one needed an ally in this gloomy house, he would certainly not be the one to turn to. Still, I wanted to find out what I could about my sister.

'I'm Miss Stewart's sister,' I said while he moved a stool over to serve as a stand for my case. His answer was a grunt that told me nothing, but I went on stubbornly. 'I wonder if she might have made some comment about her plans,' I said. 'Where she was going, for instance.'

'We didn't talk much, miss,' he said. His back was to me but I thought I detected a tone of sarcasm. It was, I was certain, unjustified. Anne was anything but snobbish. I nearly answered him sharply, but I caught myself. I didn't want to make any enemies.

'She spoke very nicely of you in her letters,' I said, thinking flattery might soften him somewhat. He ignored that tack altogether and made to leave. Thinking quickly, I said, 'Someone had to drive her into town when she left. Do you know who that would have been?'

'No, miss, I don't,' he said, waiting with obvious impatience for my interrogation to end.

'Well, aside from the family, who else is there?'

He fidgeted, obviously ill at ease. 'Just me, miss, and Mrs. Haskins.'

It was plain I was getting nowhere. I was going to pry no information out of him. 'Thank you,' I said, managing a smile despite my disappointment.

'Very good, miss,' he grunted and was gone before I had an opportunity to think of anything else.

I went to the window again, looking thoughtfully out over the lawns of the estate. A sense of discouragement came over me. I was miles from everything that was familiar to me. Before, when I was still at home and Anne was here, I had been terribly lonely, but at least my correspondence with Anne and our plans for the future had kept me cheered.

Now even those tenuous ties were gone. I was in a big old house cut off from the rest of the world. The nearest town was nearly five miles away. The bus driver had told me that little traffic used the road that came by here. There were no phones in the house; McKay had resented them as an intrusion upon his cherished privacy. Their absence and the isolation that blanketed the place had allowed him to reflect upon the world, undistracted by its clamor. He was fond of pointing out that all of the world's spiritual leaders had found it necessary to get away from the world to gain wisdom of it. Still and all, it gave me an uneasy feeling that perhaps while I was here the world would go on without me.

I had begun to remember little fragments of Anne's letters in which she had remarked about one or the other of the house's inhabitants. It was her habit to write small character sketches of people whom she met, and she had a gift for bringing them vividly to life in a few words.

Without fully realizing it I had arrived with already formed opinions of each of the people living here, shaped by Anne's remarks. Barbara Christian was unvarying in her aloofness. Grant was charming, but a mama's boy. He could not be depended upon. William Christian could most politely be described as a rake, although a very attractive one. I had just met the houseman, whose name I couldn't recall, and he was every bit as unfriendly as Anne had warned. Then there was a cook-housekeeper, Mrs. Haskins. Anne had described her personality as perfectly reflected in her bland cooking.

Anne had been genuinely fond of only Mr. McKay and his grandson. The gentleman was gone. That left, as a potential friend for me in this house, a nine-year-old boy whom I had not yet met. It was not a cheerful prospect.

While I stood at the window and considered these things briefly, I saw the houseman cross the lawn at the left of my range of vision, apparently having come from the house by a side entrance. He walked with a quick, shuffling gait and, although he was empty-handed, he moved as though carrying a great weight on his shoulders. He did not follow the drive but another path that led through some trees and brush beyond the neat lawns. I remembered a small house near where the bus had set me down; that, I presumed, was where he must live.

However, before he quitted the lawn and entered the wooded area, I saw him stop and look back, as if someone had called his name. In a minute Barbara Christian came into view, hurrying toward him. Instinctively I let the curtain fall so that I was watching through a narrow opening that they would not notice from the lawn should they happen to look my way.

I did not know why this meeting of employer and employee seemed ominous to me. There must have been a hundred reasons why she would go after the servant to catch him before he went home. As I watched, however, I saw them talk for a minute or so, and then both turned to glance up at my window. Despite the distance, I felt as though they were looking directly at me, peering through the material of the curtain to fix cold, unfriendly eyes upon me.

Involuntarily, I drew back from those looks. It was foolish; logically, she would, as a good hostess, check to see that he had brought my bag up as she had instructed, and that I was comfortable. And, since they were discussing me and my room, it was natural that they should look in my direction. Still, I could not suppress a tiny shudder that went through me.

They talked for a minute more. She seemed to be giving him instructions. Finally she dismissed him. He went on his way and, with another quick look in my direction, she came back to the house. I turned from the window and began to make myself ready for dinner.

Barbara herself came to fetch me for the evening meal. We were polite to one another, but neither of us entertained any illusions of caring for the other very much. I wondered why she had consented to my staying when she so obviously resented it. And why did she resent it so, anyway? But I did not put these questions to her directly.

The men were already at the table and they rose as we came in. Besides Grant and William, there was the boy. I saw he was a very good-looking youngster, smaller than I expected, but not exactly frail either. My immediate thought was that he would most likely grow up to be as much a heart-throb as his Uncle William was.

I also saw at once that he was shy, a condition with which I sympathize. He gave me a curious look from under lowered lashes, but when he saw me glance at him, he looked down at his shoes. I paused, expecting an introduction. To my surprise, Barbara said instead, 'You'll sit here, Miss Stewart.'

I hadn't much experience with the role of the domestic, and I supposed perhaps domestics did not always get properly introduced to family members. On the other hand, I was not a servant yet. I had not accepted that position, and for the moment I was a house guest. Admittedly I had rather thrust myself upon their hospitality; nonetheless, I had been willing to go, and I was here still because I had been invited by William to stay.

'Hello,' I said, speaking directly to the young man. 'I'm Toby Stewart, Anne's sister.'

He looked quite surprised and a little flustered by the unexpected attention. It was William Christian who remembered his manners first.

'My apologies,' he said, coming around to stand by me. 'I'm afraid I was so pleased to see you come in just now that I forgot you hadn't met my nephew. Miss Stewart, Jamie McKay.'

The boy came around the table also and gave me his hand with a mumbled 'How do you do,' that was all run together. But he gave me also a shy little smile. I thought perhaps I had made an ally.

'I came to visit my sister,' I explained, speaking to him in a grown-up fashion because I remembered how irritating I had found it at that age to be treated always as a child. 'But I'm afraid I missed her. Your family has graciously asked me to stay on and help with things here and,' I glanced at the others, 'I've decided to accept, at least for a few days until I hear from Anne. But I have to say, I'm glad you're here. This place must get a little lonely at times.'

He gave me a long look from under veiled lashes which told me more than any words could that it did indeed get lonely here for him. 'A little,' he said aloud. It was his turn to surprise me. Out of the blue, he said, 'You're awfully pretty, you know.'

Now I was flustered, but I laughed lightly. 'Thank you,' I said, making a little curtsy.

'Yes, she is, isn't she,' Grant said, to my further surprise. Despite my embarrass-ment — indeed, with no idea of doing so, I looked quickly at William, who had said nothing.

Jamie had spoken with the impetuosity of the young, and Grant with the glibness of a born flatterer, but it was the look in William's eyes that sent a thrill of excitement racing down my spine. I had never felt pretty before. I had always thought of myself as a plain, somewhat silly-looking creature. But in that moment, basking in the warmth of his gaze, I thought I knew what it was like to be beautiful.

Barbara Christian cleared her throat and said, 'Shall we sit down?' I had the honor of being assisted by two gentlemen, Jamie and William. Grant contented himself with winking at me while he held his mother's chair. Barbara was cooler than ever.

Dinner was served by Mrs. Haskins. Both it and she were as bland as I had been promised. The conversation was trivial, the sort of thing strangers talk about politely. I remember only one matter of any consequence. William asked me to call him Bill.

I thought that was rather a good idea, since I had already fallen for him.

3

Dinner was followed that first night by coffee in the den. I'd had wine at dinner, and at William's — no, Bill's — insistence, I had some brandy with my coffee. I felt a little light-headed when at last I excused myself and made my way upstairs. Whether it was the drinks or my sudden affection for Bill that intoxicated me, I could hardly have judged.

I know that my feet scarcely seemed to touch the floor; I expected any minute to go floating away into space, so light was my head. I managed a show of decorum, not wanting them to think me a silly schoolgirl, until the door of my room was closed behind me. I could restrain myself no longer, and burst into a gleeful laugh, spinning around gaily.

And there was Mrs. Haskins, staring at me in a puzzled but unexcited manner. I caught myself up short, blushing, and managed to stammer, 'What are you doing here?'

'Turning down your bed, Miss,' she said, nodding her head in that direction.

'Oh.' I felt utterly foolish. 'Thank you,' I added lamely.

'I hope you'll be comfortable,' she said, and with a nod went past me and out of the room.

My reflection looked back at me from the mirror over the dresser. I looked flushed and breathless. I stared hard at the image, willing myself sober. I had no business looking giddy and in love. I could not afford to be swept away on a tide of infatuation and forget Anne's strange disappearance. This house was ominous, and not all of Bill Christian's romantic good looks could change that fact.

I undressed and climbed thoughtfully into the big old bed. The room seemed to close in about me, and I got up to open the window and breathe deeply of the cool night air, tangy with the sea flavors. Someone downstairs was playing the piano, a Chopin waltz. The notes seemed to dance and shimmer in the darkness of the lawn. For a moment the sense of romance returned to me and I smiled at my own fears.

The music changed and became a sonata, the 'Funeral March'. My mood changed with it, and in place of romance I had a feeling of malaise. I shivered. The air was suddenly cold. I pulled the window shut and went back to bed. For a long time, however, those somber, chilling notes echoed in my memory like a knell of doom.

I dreamed of the cliffs beyond the house, those grim but awe-inspiring walls of rock against which the ocean struggled endlessly. I heard their angry roar; like a siren's song it called me. I was drawn along paths I had never seen, and suddenly I was on the sand, and the water here was a pulsing tide that rushed toward me, slowed hesitantly, paused, and then fled to re-gather its courage.

Or perhaps, I thought, it beckoned me to follow, returning for me when I lingered, and leading me out again. It whispered to me, words that I could not quite comprehend, but that had a mystic lure for me. Then, suddenly, I heard Anne's voice, calling my name. I looked, and she was the white phosphorescence of the waves.

I woke with a start, sitting up abruptly. The room was dark and cold, and for a moment completely unfamiliar. I did not know where I was, and I knew the sensation of panic. I opened my mouth to call Anne's name — and then I remembered where I was, and that Anne was not here. I took a deep calming breath, and lay back down again.

A sound at my door brought me up once more. I sat tense and frightened, staring across the dark room in that direction. 'Who's there?' I asked. My voice was strained and unnatural; I sounded even more frightened than I felt.

There was no answer. I did not want to get up and cross to the door to investigate, but on the other hand, I knew there would be no more sleep for me that night unless I did. Shivering both from the cold night air and my fright, I slipped out of the bed and padded across the room.

The hall was empty. A dim light burned at the far end, creating more shadows than it dispelled. Had I imagined the noise I heard?

Something moved near my feet. I caught a scream in my throat and jumped back, but my fright became a laugh when my would-be assailant meowed at me plaintively. 'Well hello there,' I said, kneeling to scratch a cocked ear. He was a soft yellow ball of delight who winked at me and looked me over speculatively.

'I suppose you're cold,' I said, gathering him up. 'Well, so am I, and I could use some company.'

He condescended to let me hold him until we were inside my room and the door closed. Then, with a flick of his tail, he jumped free. I waited for a moment to see if he wanted out again, but he seemed intent upon exploring the room, so I returned to bed. There, I assured myself that it had been him I heard, and that I was letting my nerves get the best of me.

I was almost asleep when he jumped onto the bed and, after an exploratory turn or two, selected a spot near my feet in which to curl up. His contented purring sent vibrations through the covers to my toes. If there were any reason for concern, he, with his allegedly more sensitive nature, slept despite it. Thinking I could do no less, I turned on my side and was soon equally fast asleep.

When I awoke next, it was morning. There was again a sound at my door, but there was nothing alarming about the energetic tap, or the bright young face that appeared when I said, 'Come in.'

'Have you seen a . . . ?' Jamie asked, and then said, 'Oh, there he is. Lucifer, you bad little cat, what are you doing in here?'

'He came calling on me during the night,' I explained. Lucifer gave each of us a disdainful look, yawned, stretched, and finally decided after all that it was time to get up. He jumped to the floor and, ignoring Jamie, strode regally into the hall.

'He must like you, then,' Jamie said. 'Or he'd never have stayed once he checked you out. He doesn't like any of the others. Except Anne. Whenever I couldn't find him in the morning, I always knew he had gone to sleep with Anne.'

'Well, I'm very flattered that Lucifer likes me. I hope he won't be the only one here who does.'

He looked down and left my hint unanswered. 'Are you really going to stay?' he asked instead.

'Yes. For a time at least,' I assured him. 'That is, so long as I'm welcome.'

'Aunt Barbara said she thought you'd be leaving,' he said, still without looking up. 'She said you'd probably go today or tomorrow.'

'Oh.' Wishful thinking, I said to myself. Aloud, I said, 'She's probably waiting to see how you and I hit it off. I'm supposed to be a companion to you, among other things.'

'A baby-sitter?' He made it sound quite unpleasant.

'Since you are hardly a baby, I don't think that would be appropriate, but people do need companions, no matter

41

how old they get.' He gave me a look that was both wary and pleased.

From outside, Lucifer complained about the delay. 'See you later,' Jamie said, and without waiting for a reply, he was gone.

The house seemed to be deserted when I came down. I reminded myself that in a house this big, people could come and go all day without necessarily seeing one another. I found my way to the dining room, and discovered that Barbara was having coffee there.

'Join me, please, won't you,' she greeted me, but with no real enthusiasm for the suggestion. 'We breakfast rather informally here. Mrs. Haskins will be in in a minute to see what you want.'

Mrs. Haskins came, in fact, almost before I had seated myself at the long table. Ordinarily I ate a big breakfast — despite a slim figure, I had an enormous appetite — but Anne had always warned me that big appetites were unladylike, and when I saw the cup of coffee and the single piece of dry toast that my hostess was having, I swallowed my hunger and asked for the same thing.

'Have you definitely decided to stay?' Barbara asked when we were alone again.

'Yes,' I answered, adding, 'that is, if the offer is still open.'

'Yes, of course,' she said.

Again, though, I had the feeling she was displeased. Why, I thought, if she so disliked having me here, did she not simply tell me to go? She was, after all, mistress of the place, and certainly a strong enough person to stand up to her son and stepson. It seemed self-evident that there was some other consideration that made her go against her own inclinations, but I could not fathom what it might be.

It crossed my mind that perhaps she, too, thought Anne's disappearance somewhat mysterious; but surely she must realize that I knew nothing about it that she did not already know. If anything, I was inclined to think she knew more than I did, in which case it was to her disadvantage to have me about.

Mrs. Haskins was back in a few

minutes with my coffee and a forlorn-looking piece of toast. She had just set it before me when Bill joined us.

'What's this?' he asked, looking at my skimpy meal. 'I'd have taken you for the bacon-and-eggs type. Don't tell me you keep that healthy glow on this kind of breakfast.' I've never been very good at concealing my feelings. He took one look at my face and chuckled. 'Take this overgrown cracker out of here,' he told Mrs. Haskins, 'and bring us both some real food. Eggs, over easy.' He glanced at me for confirmation and I nodded happily. 'And bacon — tons of it — and rolls, and butter.' He paused and looked at me again.

'And jam,' I added.

He laughed and said, 'And jam.' He pulled out a chair noisily and sat beside me. Mrs. Haskins went quietly back into the kitchen, while Barbara regarded us coolly.

'It's just as well you eat heartily,' she said. 'The weather tends to be cool here. And we've a lot of work to do today.'

'Oh, no you don't,' Bill said in an

authoritative manner. 'Not today. Today is for looking around, getting used to the place.'

'I was under the impression,' Barbara said, each word fairly dripping ice crystals, 'that Miss Stewart planned to work while she was here.'

'Oh, I do,' I said quickly.

Bill was not to be put off so easily. 'She'll work better if she has the lay of the land. My orders.' He said it with a note of finality that seemed to convince even his stepmother. She gave me a final, frosty look, and concentrated her attention on her coffee.

4

'I think,' Bill said when we had finished our hearty breakfasts and left the dining room, 'that this would be a fine time for you and your new charge to get better acquainted.'

'Yes, that would be a good idea,' I agreed, eager to do so. It occurred to me that, as Anne was fond of him also, he might be able to shed some light on her mysteriously sudden departure.

Jamie and Lucifer were out of doors, engaged in chasing butterflies. The weather had turned balmy, promising that spring was indeed on the way. The grounds about the house looked tranquil and free of any disturbing elements.

Jamie seemed to like the idea of helping escort me around. Lucifer gave us disdainful looks and went about his own business.

'The house is actually quite old, over a hundred years,' Bill explained, walking us toward the rear of the house. We were in front, where we had found Jamie.

'Funny, I had an idea Mr. McKay had built it,' I said, studying the structure. It was a big, vaguely Victorian house that rambled over the crest of the rise.

'He remodeled it extensively,' Bill explained. 'He was here nearly forty years.'

'He built right around the old house,' Jamie said, pointing. 'The old house was right in the middle — see where that window is? That was the door originally.'

'My uncle added the wings on both sides,' Bill explained. 'He liked plenty of room to get himself lost in, he said. God knows there were only the two of them until Tony — that was the son — came along.'

'That's my Dad,' Jamie added. 'And we lived here too.'

'You've always lived here, haven't you?' I asked him.

'Yes,' he said, in a voice that sounded less happy.

I gave Bill a look. 'The house belongs to Jamie,' he said. 'In trust, of course. My stepmother will stay on here to look after it.'

'But I won't be here,' Jamie said. 'She's sending me away.'

'Sending you away?' I echoed him, puzzled, and concerned at the bitterness of his tone.

'To school,' Bill explained. To Jamie, he added, 'You'll still spend vacations here. And think how much better it will be for you to be with boys your own age.'

'I like Fool's End,' he said emphatically.

'Of course you do,' I said. 'But you admitted yourself that it does get lonesome here, and it will be even more so with your grandfather gone.'

He let that remark ride and I thought it wiser not to pursue it for now, but I had an impression that there was no great love in him for his Aunt Barbara. It was a lack with which I could sympathize.

We had come about the house, still climbing gently uphill. We rounded the south corner and suddenly, so abruptly that it took the breath away, the ground fell away and the cliffs spilled down to the ocean. It was indeed dizzying, as Anne had said. I watched the waves pound at the grim gray rocks below. The water looked black and eerie.

'It's breathtaking,' I said finally.

'And a little scary, the first time,' Bill said. 'I've often wondered how it is that no one's ever fallen off these cliffs. It looks like it would be easy enough to do.'

I thought of Anne, of her sudden disappearance, and shivered. But no, Anne had been here long enough to know the cliffs were here, and dangerous. She was too practical and level-headed to take the sort of chances that could result in a fall.

'Let's go to the beach,' Jamie said, brightening.

I gave the cliffs a doubtful look. 'Not if it means going down that,' I said.

Bill laughed and said, 'There's a path over there, safe enough if you know the way.'

'I know the way,' Jamie said.

'I guess you do, as well as anybody,' Bill agreed. To me he said, 'I have to go inside, but why don't you two go on down. It's quite beautiful, actually.'

'All right,' I agreed, sorry that he wasn't going to be with us and at the same time glad that I would have an opportunity to talk more freely with Jamie.

'See you at lunch,' Bill said, and with a wave he was gone, disappearing about the house again. I watched him go and warned myself that I was being silly to feel as I did. Of course that changed my feelings not at all.

'Let's go,' Jamie said impatiently, tugging at my arm.

When I was on the path, I found myself questioning whether it was safe under any circumstances. It was scarcely more than a suggestion of a ledge that dipped down between two points and wound its way down the face of one of the cliffs. My heart was in my throat the entire descent; and yet, Jamie did indeed seem to know the way. He moved with sure-footed ease, obviously slowing his customary pace to accommodate me. I alternated between watching him admiringly, watching my feet cautiously, and eyeing the rocks below with dread.

We did finally reach the bottom,

however — hardly a beach, but rather a few scattered patches of sand between towering rocks. I wondered whether the tide was in or out, and whether the little bit of sand wasn't altogether covered up at times, but I did not want to ask and show my complete ignorance of such matters.

'If you follow the path it will take you all the way to San Francisco,' Jamie said, pointing in that general direction.

I looked, but the fact was I couldn't even see a path. 'Wonderful,' I said, supposing that to him the way led clearly across boulders and rocks where he had walked, although presumably not to San Francisco.

'Look,' he said, pointing down instead. Almost at our feet was a tide-pool, a basin of clear water left behind as the tide withdrew. We knelt together. 'It looks empty,' he said, seemingly sensing that I had little acquaintance with the ocean. 'But if you watch it for a while, you'll see all sorts of things moving around.'

It did look more or less empty to me, although there was a profusion of shells and bits of sea plants. As I watched, however, the pool began to come to life. What looked to be nothing more than a tiny shell began to walk about on the bottom. Another creature that might have been some brilliant flower in bloom swam swiftly and smoothly through the clear water. I discovered, as my vision grew accustomed to the forms of life, that the tiny basin was teeming.

'How exciting,' I murmured, staring in fascination. 'I wish Anne were here. She'd probably be able to name every one of those.'

'She knew a lot of them,' Jamie admitted.

I was suddenly brought back to the present and to the cloud that hung over my visit here. I looked up at the boy, but his face remained turned down. 'Did you come here with Anne?' I asked.

He nodded, his smile fading, as he, too, seemed to remember. 'Umm . . . humm. She spent a lot of time with me. Before my grandfather . . . when he was still here . . . the three of us came here all the time. Grandfather said you could learn everything you needed to know about people right here, watching these pools.'

'He was a very wise man,' I said. 'You must have been quite fond of him.'

'He never treated me like I was a baby,' Jamie said, in an unhappy tone that suggested others did treat him so.

'And Anne? Surely she didn't treat you like a baby. In her letters she often told me what a fine young man you were.'

He looked up at me, his young eyes clear and guileless. 'Did she really write about me?' he asked.

I nodded my head. 'Frequently. And very nice things. She liked you, you know.'

'She was nice,' he said, looking down again.

'And did you like her?'

He gave a shrug of his shoulders. 'She was all right,' he said.

I was disappointed. I had hoped for a stronger reaction, but I decided to let it ride at that for the present. 'I hope you'll decide to like me,' I said instead.

He shrugged again. After a moment he said, 'What's the use? Just about the time

I was getting to like your sister, she left. That's what always happens.'

There was a tug at my heart. I knew that I, too, would shortly be leaving, for all my efforts to befriend him. How many others had worked to gain his friendship, only to abandon him once his trust was won?

I could not believe it of Anne. I fought back the wave of emotion and forced myself to be calm. 'Anne left so suddenly,' I said. 'It was quite a surprise to me. Did she say anything about her plans? Where she was going, or why?'

He shook his head. 'She just up and left, in the middle of the night, without even saying goodbye.'

'In the middle of the night?' I repeated.

'One day she was here and the next day she was gone. She didn't even take her clothes and things with her.'

A thrill of excitement went through me. 'Are you sure?' I asked. 'It hardly seems likely she'd go off without her things.'

'She did though,' he insisted, offended that I should even question his word. 'I went to her room the next morning. Her things were still there then, but when I came down for breakfast, Aunt Barbara said she had gone.'

'But are her things still here?'

'No.'

'Did she send for them?' I could hardly contain myself. If Anne had sent for her things, then I could easily enough find out where she was.

'I guess so,' he said. 'My Aunt packed them and gave them to Carl.'

'To Carl? You're certain it was Anne's things?'

He nodded and gave me another annoyed look. I chewed at my lip thoughtfully. Carl — for that matter, the entire household — had denied any knowledge of Anne's whereabouts, but if he had sent her things on, there must have been an address.

If her things had really been sent on.

Surely, I told myself, they must have been. No woman, let alone Anne, would run away, even to elope, without taking some of her things.

If — the thought came unbidden to mind — if she had run away.

5

My tour of the estate was fairly complete that day. I saw most of the grounds; the presence of gaunt, high cliffs, the ocean vista, and a lack of close neighbors all combined to give an impression of vast space, but the grounds in fact were not extensive. There was the land on which the house sat with its wide lawn, an area of woods and brush, and a small cottage in which Carl and his wife lived.

We did not go there, but only went close enough along the path that Jamie could point out the roof to me. He could not go there, he explained, without permission. I wondered if the same would apply to me. Of course, I reminded myself, applying the philosophy I had sometimes used as a child, if I did not ask for permission, it could not be refused.

The house itself was much what it seemed. Knowing that an older structure had been remodeled, I could now distinguish between the original walls and the newer ones. The older walls were immensely thick, as much as two or three feet, so that it seemed as if a person could walk within them. I tapped and found them hollow.

'Grandfather used to tease me with stories about things hiding in the walls,' Jamie explained, in the tone of one who has long since outgrown such foolishness. 'Hiding to come out at night and frighten people.'

'I hope you weren't too frightened by such tales,' I said.

'Just when I was a kid,' he assured me.

'One hopes you have no such fears,' a male voice said behind me. I turned to see Grant Christian standing nearby. He wore a sardonic grin.

'They are thick,' I said, indicating the walls. 'All sorts of things could be in there.'

'True,' he said, coming to stand by us. 'Spanish gold, perhaps, hidden away in the dark past. Perhaps the dusty remains of some mortal being.'

Despite his joking manner, I found that

I did not like this line of conversation, nor did I consider it appropriate for Jamie who, despite his statements that he had outgrown such fears, was studying us both solemnly.

'At any rate,' I said, 'whatever is in there is certainly there to stay. Hollow or not, these walls are sturdy. And if I remember correctly, they were made hollow not to create hiding places, but to provide insulation.'

'Yes, that would be the practical explanation,' Grant said. 'Only a fanciful mind would conjure up anything more than that.'

And I was fanciful, his smile seemed to be saying. 'What I really came after you for,' he said, 'was to tell you that lunch is ready.'

I thanked him and we went quickly to clean up, but Grant Christian lingered in my mind. He seemed to be mocking me, secretly laughing at me. There was an impression that he knew secrets I did not know, and I could not help wondering whether they had anything to do with Anne.

As I came down, I encountered Mrs. Haskins in the hall; it appeared she had just come in from the garden in back. She carried a handful of herbs, and was on her way to the kitchen. 'A letter came for you, miss,' she said rather offhandedly. 'I gave it to the mistress.'

I stopped for a moment, at first puzzled and then suddenly jubilant. No one could have known I was here, and no one would be writing to me, except Anne. I could scarcely contain my excitement as I burst into the dining room where the others were already waiting. They looked at me in surprise. I had no doubt I looked a little wild-eyed, and for a moment I could hardly speak.

'You have something for me,' I said to Barbara, who viewed my excitement coldly.

'You must be mistaken,' she said, looking up and down the table with a trace of impatience. 'I believe we're ready to eat now.'

I stared at her, dumbfounded. Surely Mrs. Haskins would not have made her remark unless . . . no, she had been quite clear about it. 'A letter from my sister,' I said, standing stubbornly where I was.

'I thought I had made it clear,' Barbara said, helping herself to a fresh roll, 'I have heard nothing from your sister since she so rudely departed.'

'But a letter came for me today,' I insisted. 'And it must be from Anne.'

She did look at me then. For a moment I thought she would deny the existence of the letter. And in that moment, in that quick look she flashed at me, she answered any questions I might have had regarding her feelings for me. I had never before seen anyone literally wish me dead.

It lasted only a second or two, and was as quickly replaced by a look of surprise and chagrin. 'How silly of me,' she said, giving a short little laugh. 'I thought you were speaking of some message you thought I had received. And I completely forgot — yes, there was a letter that came for you, although I have no idea who it is from. Let me see, where did I put it?' She put a finger to her mouth, although I would have wagered everything I had that she knew exactly where that letter was.

'Oh yes, let me get it for you,' she said, standing. 'Please, everyone, go ahead. I think I left it in the library. It will only take me a minute — if it's important that you have it right now.' She directed this last at me.

'I should like to have it, yes,' I said.

She smiled and went for it. I ignored her suggestion that we go ahead with lunch and waited, standing. The others waited too. I did not look at them. I was, after all, an outsider, and I knew that in any tiff they must automatically side with Barbara. I did not want to be told, in words or looks, that I had been rude.

She was back in a minute, bearing a small white envelope. I took it from her, recognizing Anne's handwriting at once. It had been addressed to me at home, and forwarded back to me here. It had come, I saw from the return address, from this same place, Fool's End, having made a full circle to get to me.

'I should think,' Grant said, interrupting the silence, 'that after such a fuss, the least you could do is open it and share it with us.'

'Certainly,' Barbara said with barely concealed sarcasm. 'After all, lunch could hardly get any colder than it is by this time.'

I looked and found Bill's eyes gentle and sympathetic. 'Why don't you go on into the library and read it,' he said softly but firmly. 'It may be important. We'll go ahead with lunch.'

'Thank you,' I said gratefully. 'Excuse me,' I said to the room in general, and left them, walking with head high.

My hands were shaking so badly by the time I reached the library that I could hardly get the letter open. I tore the single sheet of paper from the envelope and unfolded it. Anne's neat, precise handwriting jumped out at me.

'Toby Dearest,' it read, 'I know that this will disappoint you, but I'm writing to ask you — no, to demand — that you not come to Fool's End as we planned. I can't explain it all just now. I don't think I understand it all myself, and in any event, I want to get this in the mail to you before your plans get too far along. Later I'll try to fill you in on all the details. For now it will have to suffice to say that there are things very wrong here. Just how wrong I don't know yet, but I mean to find out. Take care, pet, and wait patiently until you hear from me.'

It was signed simply, 'Anne.' I looked at the date. It was written two days before Anne supposedly left Fool's End. Things were wrong here, 'very wrong.' And she had intended to learn more. She did not want me to come to Fool's End. Because of danger? She had written a brief, hurried note asking me not to come until she learned . . . something.

Two days later she was gone, disappeared as if from the face of the earth. Gone, leaving no forwarding address, no message of any kind. Gone, leaving behind her clothes, her personal things, her suitcase. Gone, without a trace.

And it was I who was at Fool's End now, trying to learn, as she had tried to learn, what was wrong here.

I folded the letter neatly, my hands no longer shaking. I put it back in its envelope and dropped it into the deep pocket of my skirt. Then, surprising even myself with my outward show of nonchalance, I came back to the dining room.

It looked as if no one had done more than pick at their food. I summoned up a smile and sent it around the table. 'What's this?' I said, looking down at Jamie's plate. 'If my being here is going to affect your appetite like that, I'm certain to be sent away promptly.' He gave me a cautious smile and began to eat again.

'I promise to exert all of my influence to keep you here,' Grant said, holding my chair for me. Bill, who had stood, gave me a look that was full of questions I could not quite read.

'Well,' Barbara said when I was seated, 'I hope you don't mean to keep us in suspense for the entire day. Wasn't I right? Didn't Anne elope?'

'No, she didn't elope,' I said without looking up — I could not trust my face not to betray me. 'At least, she makes no mention of it in her letter.'

'Then where is she?' Grant asked.

'She was still here when the letter was written,' I said.

'Then you still don't know where she

is?' Barbara asked.

I would have liked to lie, but I was certain the truth would be apparent in my face and voice. 'No,' I said. 'She makes no mention of any plans to leave Fool's End.'

'Certainly a secretive one, wasn't she,' Barbara said, as though concluding the subject.

'No,' I said, more sharply than I should have. 'She wasn't, at least not with me. And I for one would like very much to know where she is, and why she went.'

'So would we all,' Grant said.

My eyes went again to Bill, but he was not looking at me. His attention was concentrated on his food. He had not asked questions about the letter, or about Anne's whereabouts. Perhaps he was being considerate. Or perhaps he simply didn't care.

Or, I found myself thinking, perhaps he didn't ask because he already knew the answer.

6

I was scarcely able to eat the food before me. If Mrs. Haskins's food had seemed bland before, it was odious now. The dark walls of the house seemed to close in about me. I had the sensation that all of them were watching me, and I dared not look up to meet their glances. After a decent interval, I excused myself and went to my room, but there was no sense of safety even there.

Something had been wrong here. Something had frightened Anne badly enough for her to warn me away from the place. Where had she gone, and why? Yet while these questions were frightening me, they were simultaneously strengthening my resolution. I would not run away, despite the fervent temptation to do so. Something had happened to my sister, something bad enough that it was being concealed from me. And I was determined to learn what that something was.

Fool's End had become a house of mystery, but I vowed, standing at the window looking over the lawns and the woods at their edge, that I would solve that mystery before I left.

As I stood at the window, thinking over these things, a flash of color caught my attention. A bright red sports car shot into view on the road. It slowed with a whining sound, turned onto the drive, and shot up toward the house, its engine roaring. It was long and low and sleek, and needed no price tag on it to tell you that it had cost a pretty penny when purchased. It came to an abrupt halt in a cloud of dust, and so quickly that it seemed the car had scarcely died when a woman alighted from the driver's side.

Even from this distance I could see that she was beautiful — exquisitely beautiful, in fact, with the sort of beauty every woman, no matter how plain, sometimes pretends to herself that she has. Like her car, she was long and sleek and expensive-looking, and she moved with arrogant grace and power. Her hair was coppery colored, her pants suit green, her walk purposeful. She was not the sort another woman would want to compete with, in any contest. There was an impression that she would win whatever prize she went after, by whatever means.

I would have liked to avoid this lovely creature's presence. It has always been my experience that such people only increase my own clumsiness and make me all the more ill at ease and unsure of myself. Nevertheless, I was curious, too, for more reasons than one. In the first place, if I meant to learn anything about Anne's disappearance, I would have to be alert to everything that went on. In the second place, I wondered whom she had come to visit.

So I went downstairs again, after first taking a disappointing look in the mirror. The family was in the library, and presumably the visitor with them. I paused at the door, and my heart sank even lower. Close, this visitor was even lovelier. Her hair was like a coppery cloud that floated about her pale, exquisitely sculptured face. Her eyes were so dark that they might have been onyx, giving her an arresting look. She was slim, but not with my own gangly slimness; the curves she had were all exactly where they were supposed to be for maximum effect.

And as if all this were not enough, she was with Bill. Not just with him, but *with* him. They held hands, their arms linked, and she was leaning against him in a manner that negated the possibility of mere friendship, but rather declared something much more than that.

She turned those dark eyes on me as I paused in the doorway, and gave me a look that was penetrating and cold. She seemed to weigh me in that one glance, and find me wanting. When she looked away, I felt as though I had been literally tossed over her shoulder as one would discard a used tissue or the core of an eaten apple. I hadn't even the heart to look at Bill; I felt pretty certain what I would see in his handsome eyes.

'And this,' the beautiful one was saying, 'is the visiting relative, I presume?' Her tone suggested that I was a charity case that the family had taken in, and I felt my cheeks sting and redden.

'Toby's graciously consented to stay on a few days and give us a hand with things,' Bill said quickly. 'Toby Stewart, Glenda Adams. Glenda is a neighbor of sorts.'

Bill's literal charity did little to make me feel better. I stammered, 'How do you do,' and held out my hand.

She ignored it. 'If you can call twenty miles away being neighbors,' she said with a throaty laugh. She clung more closely to Bill and looked up at him with those dark eyes of hers. 'It doesn't matter, though. I'll travel any distance for what I want.'

I looked for the first time since entering the room at Bill, and was surprised to find his eyes on me. His face was expressionless, but I could not help but think that he saw my anguish. I bit my lip and berated myself for being so utterly foolish. Not five minutes before, I had been facing the fact that something unpleasant must have happened regarding my sister, and that the Christians were responsible for whatever that something was. Now I was trying to swallow a lump in my throat because one of the

70

Christians was infatuated — and it must be infatuation; she was not the sort of girl men really fell in love with — with someone else.

'I thought,' I said aloud, 'that I would rather like some work to do today after all. I've spent enough time in idleness.'

'Well, I haven't,' Glenda announced. 'And neither have you, darling,' she added, speaking to Bill. 'I've hardly seen you the last few days. Pretty soon I'll suspect you of having an affair with Miss Stewart here.' She laughed, showing more than the usual complement of white teeth, to indicate how preposterous she thought that suggestion was. 'I absolutely insist that you come with me. I have scores of things that I want to pick up in town, and I need someone big and strong to carry them for me.'

I wanted badly to ask if her shopping list included a fresh supply of venom, but I checked myself.

'Come along,' Barbara said to me. 'I'll show you where to begin.'

I followed her from the room. Behind me I heard Bill say, 'I'll go and change, and meet you at the car.' I did not look back. I supposed he was kissing her, and I didn't care to see her tail wagging with happiness.

Barbara took me to what was obviously Walter McKay's office. Despite the time that had passed since his death, it had an appropriate air of clutter. The desk was a battered old affair that seemed to reflect him more accurately than the more elegant furnishings of the rest of the house. I could easily imagine him seated in this room, his feet probably up on the desk, the same haphazard-looking stacks of papers scattered all about him. The air seemed charged with his presence still.

'It's lovely,' I said, more to myself than to Barbara.

She gave me a peculiar look. 'You think so?' she asked, in a tone that suggested she had no high opinion of my taste in rooms. 'I'm afraid it's rather cluttered. My brother was not a very neat man, as you can see. It was a full-time job trying to keep things looking right when he was around.'

I did not remark how trivial a little

clutter must have seemed to him, living as he did in the splendid halls and lovely rooms of his own mind. She would not have understood, of that I was certain. She had lived with the man, she even had the same blood in her veins, but she obviously had never known him.

The work was little more than a sorting and cataloguing job. There were entire cartons of papers — some of them full letters, some of them nothing more than scraps on which he had scribbled some note. There was a file for new material — of which there was apparently very little — and a file which contained records of his previous writings, and against which any suspect material could be checked. I could see that Anne's knowledge of his writings would have been an invaluable asset, without which the job might have taken years, and I was grateful that I, too, was familiar with them.

'Most of it, I'm afraid, is nothing more than trash,' Barbara said unhappily. 'I had hoped that there might be enough to justify another publication, but it hardly seems likely. Still, we can't afford to pass up the possibility, I suppose.'

She left me to work with the 'trash.' It was as pleasant a way as I could think of to pass an afternoon, and even my unhappiness over the intimacy between Bill and Glenda was relegated to a distant corner of my consciousness.

It came to the fore once when, a few minutes after I had begun, Bill himself came into the room. I looked up and blushed when I saw him, and looked quickly back at my work.

'Finding everything all right?' he asked.

'Yes,' I said simply.

When it became apparent that I was going to offer nothing more, he said, 'I'm afraid it's not a very exciting way to spend your time.'

'On the contrary,' I said without looking up, 'it's most enjoyable. Of course, it's a question of what one enjoys. For me, shopping all afternoon would only be a chore.'

I was sorry as soon as I had added that, but if he minded, he did not say so. After another silence, he said, 'You know, I never really read anything of his. I suppose if the truth were known, I always sort of resented his being so great and wise and all that, while I was such a worthless bounder.'

I looked up then, surprised, and said, too quickly and too vehemently, 'I would hardly call you that.'

I blushed, and he smiled. 'But,' he said, very softly, 'you don't really know me, of course.'

And he was right. I did not know him. Not at all.

After a moment he left, but as he went out of the door, he said, 'Thank you anyway.'

I quickly buried myself in the papers before me, determined to put him out of my mind. After all, what was he to me? He was a handsome man with a charming manner, that was all. And I was insane to fancy myself in love with him. It was only that, of all the people I had met here, he was the only one who seemed genuinely kind and concerned about me. He took more of an interest in Jamie than the others, which was certainly to his credit.

I stubbornly thrust aside all thoughts of

him and went back to my work. It was fascinating, and required one's full attention, so that it was not hard to forget the questions that haunted my mind. So I was surprised, when Jamie interrupted me, to discover that almost two full hours had elapsed. I had been unaware of anything but McKay's notes. Jamie paused timidly just inside the room, waiting to see if I would notice him. I looked up at once and gave him a welcoming smile.

'Hello. Join me, won't you?' I said. 'It's a little lonesome here.'

'I'm not supposed to be in here,' he said, remaining where he was.

'Probably your grandfather was afraid you'd disarrange things,' I said. 'But it can't matter much now.'

'Oh, Grandfather liked to have me here with him. It's Aunt Barbara that said I couldn't come here since Grandfather died.'

I nearly said something angry, but I managed not to do so. Barbara was, after all, the boy's guardian, and I had no right to interfere with her instructions to him. But it seemed to me that the boy must miss his grandfather a great deal, and it seemed cruel to deny him the comfort of coming here where, apparently, the two had spent part of their time together.

'Well,' I said, standing, 'if you can't join me, then why don't I join you? I could use a breath of air. My brain seems to be working even slower than usual. Let's have a stroll, shall we?'

Outside, however, the air had turned chilly. 'You wait here,' I said, 'while I run upstairs and get myself a sweater. I'll only be a minute.'

I left him on the front steps and hurried up to my room. I took a sweater from the drawer in which I had put them, and was about to close the drawer when something struck me as odd. It was hardly a specific fact, but more of an impression, that things had been moved. I stared at the drawer's contents for a full minute. I could not put my finger on it, but I was certain, the longer I looked, that they were slightly rearranged from the way I had put them.

What could that mean? There was nothing in the drawer of any value;

nothing of particular value, as a matter of fact, in any of my things: some inexpensive clothes, a few pieces of costume jewelry, a few personal items.

I closed that drawer and opened the one above it. It, too, had an air of having been cautiously disturbed.

It was then I remembered the letter. It was gone from where I had left it, under a stack of handkerchiefs. I looked swiftly through the drawer, moving things about roughly, and then I looked again more carefully. I searched the other drawers too, although I was certain of where it had been.

It was really gone.

And as I stood, staring into space, I became aware of something else, something so subtle that I had been only vaguely aware of it since I had come into the room. It was a scent at once seductive and masculine, and I recognized it as the cologne that Bill Christian wore. Faint though it was, I was certain once I had identified it.

He had been in my room, and had taken the letter from Anne.

7

I argued with myself as I went back down to join Jamie. Bill had been gone nearly two hours. His scent could not have lingered in my room for that length of time. Yet I was certain beyond any shadow of a doubt that it was the scent he wore. It was different from what Grant usually had on. It was the sort of peculiar little thing I had a tendency to notice about a man, the way he smelled. And about one thing my imagination was most certainly not playing any tricks: Someone had taken Anne's letter, and the possibilities were few: Barbara, Grant, Bill, Mrs. Haskins or Carl.

I was in the downstairs hall before I saw Bill. I was so surprised that I stopped short, staring. He laughed and said, 'Does my appearance startle you so badly?'

'I thought you were out,' I stammered.

'I was. But the shopping took less time

79

than was expected. I decided you were right.'

'About what?'

'It is an unpleasant chore.' He seemed to notice my consternation and asked, 'Is anything wrong? You look like you've seen a ghost.'

I shook my head extravagantly. 'No, nothing,' I said. I went by him, cutting off any further conversation, and out the door.

He must have come back while I was working, without my noticing. He could have indeed been in my room within the last few minutes, recently enough for the scent of his cologne to linger. And just now I had confirmed what I had already been certain of — that it was his cologne.

Jamie was waiting for me. We walked to the woods that ringed the property, and followed a path that he seemed to know. Here the air was thick with the scent of pine, juniper, and what else I did not know. The ground was a soft carpet underfoot, already fresh and green with spring.

Jamie chattered, much freer with me

than he had been before. He seemed not to notice my preoccupation and I made an effort to answer his questions and encourage his talkativeness, but my thoughts were really elsewhere.

I had decided, by the time we returned to the house, to make no mention of the missing letter. Perhaps that would encourage whoever had taken it to become more careless the next time. It was in one of Walter McKay's books that I had once read that we learn more about a person by his mistakes than by the things he does perfectly. It was perhaps just as well for me that his relatives were less familiar with his work than I.

Dinner was much as it had been the night before. Barbara was aloof toward me, Grant flirtatious in a harmless manner, and Bill pleasant but somewhat distant. He seemed preoccupied and I tried not to think that it was because he had stolen a letter from my room.

Barbara did offer one bit of news. 'I have decided to have a dinner party,' she said halfway through the meal. 'We've done no entertaining since Walter died, and we do owe a great many invitations.'

Neither of the men seemed to attach any particular importance to this announcement. 'I'll leave it all in your capable hands,' was all Grant said, and Bill said nothing, merely shrugging it off as of no particular consequence. My presence at this event was not mentioned, and I rather doubted that Barbara would care to invite an employee, particularly one of which she was not fond.

The combination of fresh air and salt water, and no doubt the strain under which I had been all day, left me ready for bed at an early hour. Once there, despite the questions that plagued me, I fell asleep almost at once.

When I woke it was dark, the middle of the night. I thought at first that Lucifer the cat had come again to disturb my sleep, and I padded across the floor in my bare feet to open the door.

He was nowhere in sight. Thinking that he had simply wandered down the hall a little distance, I stepped out and went a few feet toward the stairs.

Only gradually did I become aware of the changing shadows. They came and went, flickering, as though ghosts played upon the stairs. Finally I realized that they were the result of lights that moved about downstairs.

I ran a hand over my eyes, trying to brush away the vestiges of sleep. I had no idea what hour it was, and impelled by curiosity, I went back to my room to look at my watch where I had left it on the night stand. It was three a.m.

I went back to the hall, and to the head of the stairs, realizing that by snooping in the middle of the night I could be inviting dismissal. Not that the job meant that much to me, but the mystery of Anne's disappearance did.

I thought at first that the lights were gone, and was halfway down the stairs before I saw them again. The mysterious play of light and shadow had been the result of flashlights, seemingly shielded to make their beams less conspicuous. They came from McKay's office, and as I came closer there was a murmur of voices, too low to distinguish what they said or to whom they belonged.

Why should the residents of this house be searching Walter McKay's office in the middle of the night, with flashlights? It seemed incredible to me. If it were not any of the Christians, however, who could it be?

A sound behind and above me, on the stairs, gave me a start. I whirled about. Something moved in the darkness at the top of the stairs, scurrying out of sight. I had a moment of terror and the thought that I was surrounded by shadowy enemies whom I did not know nor could even see.

I angrily shoved that feeling aside. I was not going to be frightened out of my wits like some schoolgirl, and I was not going to be followed about in the dark either. I went quickly up the stairs. I saw nothing there, but as I paused there was another burst of motion before me, where the hall met the other that ran across the house. I ran in that direction, but again I saw nothing; and though I listened with my senses straining, I heard nothing more.

I started back to continue my investigation of the activity downstairs — and ran straight into the arms of Bill Christian. He stepped from an open door so suddenly that I could not help but literally step into his open arms. I nearly screamed, but somehow I caught the sound in my throat, and it became a gasp instead.

'Up rather late, aren't you?' he asked. He wore a mocking smile, but I had an impression he found this meeting no more amusing than I did.

'I thought I heard something,' I managed to say, my voice sounding tremulous even to my own ears. I was frightened and embarrassed.

For a moment I was certain that he meant to kiss me, and my fright did not prevent my lips from parting in an instinctive acceptance of that kiss. Unfortunately — or perhaps fortunately — it never came. Instead, he released me so suddenly that I swayed off balance.

'I didn't hear a thing,' he said. 'Probably just the wind playing tricks. An old house like this can make a lot of noises of its own. When you're used to it, you don't hear them at all, but for a newcomer they can be eerie.'

I wanted to ask him why he was up at this strange hour if he had heard nothing, or if it had been him downstairs with a flashlight, but I did not trust my voice. I nodded and backed away from him in the direction of my own room.

'You ought not to be running around the house like this at night,' he said. 'It could be dangerous.' I must have looked even more frightened at that, because he added, 'You could stumble on the stairs. Not to mention the risk of colds. That's not a very warm outfit you've got on.'

My face went crimson as I realized that I was wearing nothing but a flimsy nightgown. 'Good night,' I whispered hoarsely, aware that my embarrassment had brought a chuckle to his lips. I turned and fled to my room, breathing heavily once the door was closed after me.

Something brushed against my bare leg. My hand flew to my mouth to stop my scream. A plaintive meow from below told me I had company. I laughed at my own fears and bent down to pick up the yellow ball of fluff. 'You certainly gave me a start,' I said, cuddling him against my cheek. 'Tell me, did they disturb your sleep too, those mysterious prowlers?'

If he were concerned about any prowlers, he gave no evidence of the fact. He purred contentedly in my arms, and in a minute I carried him back to bed with me and pulled the covers over both of us.

Sleep did not come so easily this time. I lay listening to the sounds of the night. Bill had told some truth, at least: the house did have a symphony of noises all its own — some ominous, some quite innocent-sounding. I came to recognize certain regular creaks and the faint distant rattle of a loose shutter, and a scurrying that indicated mice in the attic above. I heard no sounds, however, to match those I had heard before, from below. Someone had been down there; someone had been searching. And Bill Christian knew that as well as I did. Else why would he have been abroad at three in the morning, in pajamas and robe and slippers?

Who had it been, then, in the office below? Bill himself? There had been time enough for him to come up the stairs after me, but why should he search like a phantom in the night? And no more should the others, when any of them could search to their heart's content by broad daylight.

And for what had they been searching?

What was more, if it had been the Christians who searched below, who had been following me?

★ ★ ★

I slept badly and woke to one of those gray mornings that so frequently accompany spring in California. There was no real threat of rain, only a dismal negation of the sun which matched my mood perfectly.

I had scarcely reached the dining room when Bill followed me in. Barbara was already there, having her toast and coffee. Grant, I had concluded, was not an early riser most mornings.

'I trust everyone slept well,' Barbara said, with no real display of interest.

'Like a log,' Bill said. He was behind her, where she could not see the glance he threw at me. 'How about you, Toby?'

'Beautifully,' I lied, not knowing why I should do so for his sake, and yet doing so without even pausing to consider it.

I tried to eat my customary generous breakfast, not wanting Bill to see how disturbed I was, but I could manage to do little more than pick over the food, and I was glad when he excused himself and went out. I left the dining room soon after him.

I had made up my mind that I wanted to talk to the hired man, Carl, again. Jamie had said that Barbara had packed Anne's things and given them to Carl, which meant that he must know more than he had told me the first time, and I intended to pin him down.

Of course, I could hardly explain all this to Barbara. All I could do was wander about outside the house in the hope that I would see him and have an opportunity to confront him.

Fortunately, I did not have long to wait. Soon after I had strolled outside, he came about the house from the direction of the garages, carrying a bulky tool case. I did not waste time trying to establish a rapport with him; our previous encounter led me to think that any such attempt would be unsuccessful. Instead, I put myself boldly in his path and waited for him.

He avoided looking at me until he was right in front of me, as though he hoped I might weaken and just go away. Finally, though, he stopped in front of me and gave me a hostile look, waiting silently for me to explain what I wanted.

'I'm still trying to find where my sister might have gone,' I said, coming right to the point.

'I told you, she didn't say anything to me,' he growled, looking even less friendly than before. His face darkened and his eyes looked menacing.

'I was told that Mrs. Christian brought her suitcase to you the day after she left,'

I said, refusing to back down before his malevolent stare.

'That's a lie,' he said. 'I never saw no suitcase. Whoever told you that was lying.'

'If you sent the suitcase on for her, you must have had an address,' I insisted, ignoring his accusation. In a coaxing tone, hoping to soften his resentment of me, I added, 'Don't you see how important this is to me? You're the only one who might know where . . . '

'I don't know nothing,' he said, so angrily and with such emotion that I half expected him to lift a hand and strike me on the spot. 'Anybody who says different is a liar, that's all.' With that, he went by me and hurried on his way without so much as a backwards glance. I stood where I was for a moment, shaking with anger and frustration.

I took a deep breath to calm myself, and thought. What exactly had Jamie told me? Not, upon reflection, that he had actually seen the suitcase handed from Barbara to Carl. Very well, I would make certain of that one point before I went any further. I did not want to alarm Jamie unduly, though. Sooner or later he would be down to see me this morning; I sensed that he was growing quite fond of me, as I already was fond of him. There would be time enough then to question him upon this and upon another point that had occurred to me during the night.

I had been at work only a short time when Grant came into the room in which I worked. I was surprised when he informed me that Barbara's dinner party was for the following evening.

'I hadn't expected to join in,' I said frankly.

'But what is a dinner party without a lovely young woman at my side?' he asked in a mocking tone.

'I suspect the neighborhood can provide ample loveliness,' I replied. Then, remembering something, I said, 'There is a favor I'd like to ask of you, by the way.'

'Your slightest wish will be my command,' he said.

'I would like to have Jamie with me while I work. He might be able to help a little, and in any case it would be company for both of us. But he tells me he's been forbidden to come into this room.'

'So, you'd rather have another man at your side?' he cocked an eyebrow and assumed a wounded look. I could not help but smile at his nonsense. He relented and shrugged. 'Well, so be it. If it's him you love, him you'll have. Leave everything to me.'

He left and I was thoughtful for a moment. It was not difficult to be amused by Grant, even charmed by him. I doubted that I could ever take any of his attentions seriously, although I had no doubt that plenty enough girls were willing to do so. But the point was, it was difficult to think of Grant in a sinister manner. He seemed altogether harmless, discounting the breaking of a few hearts from time to time.

My thoughts were interrupted by Jamie's arrival. He was quite pleased when I told him that I had gotten permission for him to work with me if he wished. I felt again, and keenly, the boy's loneliness and his eagerness to have a friend.

'However,' I said firmly, 'I have a tendency to sit and chatter, so you'll have the responsibility of seeing that we stick to the job. If the work doesn't progress, you know, I'll be out on my ear.'

He was pleased to have the role of the firm hand and he took to the work with a seriousness that was touching and charming. I found that the work did indeed go faster with his help. Moreover, he was not ignorant regarding his grandfather's work. He was able to identify many bits and scraps almost immediately. An elusive fragment that I might have spent hours upon was explained away quickly as, 'Oh, that was a thought that occurred to him one day when we were talking. He wrote it down because he thought it would make a good story if he developed it.' And again, 'That comes from his book of essays. He didn't remember having written it, and thought it was kind of clever.'

'Oh, look,' he said at one juncture, handing me a sheet of paper, 'here's a note of your sister's.'

I took it and looked. My sister had

written an identifying note at the bottom of the page. It was only the name of McKay's book from which the quote was taken, but the sight of her handwriting gave my heart a pang.

It gave me, too, the opportunity for broaching the matter that was on my mind. 'I asked Carl about Anne's suitcase,' I said, trying to sound as nonchalant as possible. 'But he said you must have been mistaken; that he had never seen any such thing.'

He was silent for a while, and when I glanced at him I saw at once the conflict on his young face. He was struggling within himself, trying to decide if he dared challenge Carl's statement without putting himself in the wrong.

'I'll believe whatever you tell me,' I said softly, putting a hand upon his. 'I only want to be certain of the facts. Did you actually see the case handed to him?'

He nodded, timidly at first and then with ferocity. 'Yes,' he said firmly. 'He's telling a lie. I saw my aunt carry the suitcase out of the house, and he took it and went off with it down to his place.'

'Then I suppose he's forgotten,' I said, but the explanation sounded as hollow to my ears as it must have to his. I did not believe Carl had forgotten. He had lied.

And the implications of that fact were frightening.

8

Although I mulled it over for the rest of the morning, I could think of no tactful or subtle way of broaching the other question that was on my mind, and finally I decided simply to seize the bull by the horns.

'Jamie,' I said when conversation provided me an opening, 'the room I'm in was not my sister's room, was it?'

He gave me a quizzical look. 'No, why?'

I left his question unanswered. 'Can you show me which room was my sister's?' I asked.

He nodded. He did not again ask why. I think he had begun to suspect.

'Take me there now,' I said, standing. 'I'd like to see it, just out of curiosity.'

He got up too, wordlessly, and led the way out of the room. I did not have to suggest that we be cautious; he seemed to understand that we did not want to share this little expedition with others.

The room to which he led me was easily identifiable as the one Anne had described to me in her letters. From the windows one did indeed seem to be suspended over the cliffs and the turbulent waters. Even with the windows closed, the tumult of the waves filled the room with an ominous rumble.

But there was no clue to Anne's disappearance. While Jamie watched me with a steady stare, I searched through the drawers of the dresser, and through the closets, but with no success. Her things were gone, as was she. I went to the window and pulled back the curtain to gaze down at the ocean below.

I had found no clues. I was surrounded by people I could not trust. A wave of despondency swept over me, just as the waves below swept over the bleak rocks.

'Look,' Jamie exclaimed suddenly, breaking into my thoughts. He pointed. 'There,' he said, 'under the chair.'

I stooped, and saw what had caught his attention — a glimmer of gold. I brought it out and held it in the palm of my hand while he bent over my shoulder to see. It was a locket, small and of no practical value, but its sentimental value was immeasurable. It had belonged to our mother and she had given it to Anne as a keepsake when Anne had been only sixteen. It had been Anne's most precious possession. I could not imagine Anne leaving the locket behind, even under a chair — unless she had left against her will, or so suddenly that she had no time to look for it.

'You're worried about your sister, aren't you?' Jamie asked. 'Are you afraid?'

I realized that I might be alarming him. 'Just a little puzzled,' I said, giving him a wan smile.

He put a hand on my shoulder. 'Don't worry,' he said in a man's voice, 'I'll protect you.'

'With such support, you ought to feel perfectly safe.'

It was so unexpected that we both jumped nearly a mile, both my protector and I. Neither of us had heard Bill come into the room, but there he stood behind us, just inside the doorway.

I stood quickly, putting a protective

arm about Jamie's shoulders. 'You startled me,' I said.

'I'm sorry,' he said, and looked as though he meant it. 'I didn't mean to eavesdrop, and the last thing on this earth I'd want to do would be to frighten you unnecessarily.'

I softened at his apparent sincerity. 'I guess I was just too jumpy. I'm not sure we ought to be in here.'

'Why not? It was your sister's room.' He glanced around it as if seeing it for the first time. 'I'm surprised Barbara didn't put you in here. Maybe she thought the view would frighten you. The ocean is a bit wild here.'

I nearly explained that I had originally asked to be put in this room, but I checked myself and said nothing. It would be too easy for me to trust this man; my heart begged me to do so, but my head warned me otherwise. I hadn't a single reason for trusting him, and several reasons for not doing so.

He changed the subject rather abruptly. 'My brother mentioned that you weren't planning on joining us tomorrow night.

Did you have other plans?'

'I think you know that I don't,' I said, smiling. 'Where else would I be going?'

He smiled too. 'I was very much counting on your being there.'

'I can't imagine what difference it would make whether I am there or not,' I said.

'It will make a great deal of difference to me,' he said.

I had a feeling that he could read all of the emotions that flitted across the landscape of my mind. I could only say, 'Then surely I must change my mind and join you.'

He smiled — little grasping what it did to my already overtaxed heart — and said, 'Thank you.'

He left and for a moment I stared after him in breathless excitement until I again became aware of Jamie's presence. And from remembering Jamie, I went to remembering the locket in my hand. How could I be so completely in love with a man who, unless all of the indications were wrong, was somehow involved in my own sister's disappearance? The fact that she had left behind her precious locket signified to me that I was right to be afraid for her.

And whatever had happened to her — and I could only guess at it — might as easily happen to me also.

* * *

Jamie had enough breeding and good manners not to question me about Bill. Once or twice during the afternoon, which he spent working with me, I saw him giving me puzzled glances, but I pretended not to see them. We took refuge from one another and ourselves in the work, and the afternoon went quickly.

Before dinner we took a stroll. At the path that led to Carl's cottage, I was tempted to pay a visit there. I knew he had a wife and I wondered if she might not be friendlier than he, but I remembered that Jamie could not go there without permission, and decided that I would make that visit on another occasion.

After dinner, which was uneventful, I retired to my room. I had been thinking ahead to the next evening's dinner party. I had brought nothing with me suitable for a grand occasion. On the other hand, I was good with a needle, and among the things I had brought with me was an old dress of Anne's that I had been meaning to make over, since it was too good simply to discard, and she could no longer wear it. It was expensive silk, and a shade of blue that set off my complexion and my golden hair to perfection.

I had been working for nearly an hour when Mrs. Haskins came in to turn down the bed. I was surprised when she complimented me. 'That's very pretty, miss,' she said.

'Thank you,' I answered. 'Oh I wonder, maybe you could help me with it for a minute. I need someone to pin it while I try it on.'

She seemed pleased to be asked, and it occurred to me that life must be very lonely here for her, too. It was no wonder that she was so bland, with no one to talk to, nothing to do with her time. While we worked, I made an effort to get information from her.

'I've been worried about my sister,' I said cautiously. 'She left so mysteriously, and no one seems to know why, or for where. I don't suppose you can shed any light on the matter?'

She shook her head and put a pin neatly in place. 'No, miss. People don't talk to me much.'

I was disappointed, but not surprised. After a minute she ventured another remark. 'She left sudden like,' she said, finished with the pinning. 'Didn't even take her things with her.'

'That seems odd,' I said. 'Are you certain?'

'I was in the next morning to straighten up,' she said indignantly. 'The missus was packing them for her. She said the young lady had left during the night.'

So, I thought, Jamie's story of the suitcase was confirmed. For a minute I toyed with the idea of going to Barbara and confronting her with the story, until I remembered how she had tried to deceive me regarding Anne's letter. At the very least I would cause trouble for Mrs. Haskins.

As I prepared for bed that night, I thought of the strange goings on the night before. I wondered if they would occur again tonight, and whether I dared risk looking into them again.

It was nearly two when I woke. This time I thought to don a robe and slippers. I opened my door a crack and listened. All of the sounds were from below. The upstairs hall was deserted.

I came down the stairs noiselessly and hesitated at their foot. This time there was no light to tell me where they were. I could hear the murmur of voices, sounding now distant, now close, but it was as if they were the voices of phantoms drifting on the night air. I crept down the hall, trying to pinpoint the direction of the sound.

I nearly screamed as a thump echoed near me, almost at my side. It seemed to come from the wall itself, and for a minute I thought of ghosts, almost believing that the place was haunted after all.

Then I remembered what I had been told of the original house with its three-foot thick, hollow walls — in which, as Grant Christian had told me with some amusement, the mortal remains of a human being might be hidden. I had a sudden, horrifying vision of Anne sealed within those walls, perhaps even now trying to communicate with me. I nearly knocked on the wall in answer, but common sense came to the fore. If Anne had been locked in those walls since her disappearance, she would no longer be knocking on them.

Before I could consider the matter further, I heard a sound above. Alarmed, I moved into the darkness of an open doorway, the door to the dining room, and watched. In a moment, Bill Christian came stealthily down the stairs. He paused at the bottom, listening, and I held my breath as if he might hear that sound. Then, still moving warily, he went into McKay's office.

I dared not risk remaining where I was. I was certain that being found spying like this would mean trouble for me, and as soon as he had gone inside, I darted for the stairs.

As I neared the top, I heard once again the scurrying sound I had heard the night before, and ahead of me, where the two halls crossed, I had a glimpse of white disappearing about a corner.

I ran there, but there was nothing in sight. There were too many rooms in which someone could hide. The house was too big and too rambling. I could chase phantoms all night, like will-o'-the-wisps, and never meet one face to face.

I moved cautiously down the hall, looking from side to side, but I saw nothing. I stopped halfway along, ready to admit that my search was futile. For a moment I stood where I was.

I heard a noise behind me, the creak of a floorboard, then another, close together, as if someone were running toward me, but the movement was so swift that before I had time to turn, to scream, to escape, a powerful hand had seized me and I was jerked violently about.

9

I found myself looking with frightened eyes into the angry face of Bill Christian.

'What are you doing out here?' he demanded in a low voice.

'I . . . I heard noises again,' I stammered.

For a moment he looked as though he wanted to shake me. Then, taking my hand in his strong grip, he nearly dragged me back to the door of my room.

'For God's sake, stay in there at night,' he said, letting me go. 'I have enough to worry about without wondering whether you're going to get your pretty neck broken. Stop snooping, do you hear me?'

I could only nod dumbly. Then, as if I weren't in enough of a turmoil already, he seized me again, this time in both of his arms, and gave me the kiss I had expected the night before. My heart threatened to explode as his lips sought and found mine, and kissed them ferociously. Then, as quickly as it had begun, it was over. 'Please, do as I say,' he said in a more gentle tone.

I was still speechless. I merely nodded again, and went inside, closing my door after myself.

I threw myself across my bed, in a delirium of conflicting emotions.

★   ★   ★

I woke from sleep with a smile on my face and the memory of Bill's kiss on my mind. After a moment, though, the smile faded, and I grew sober. Things at Fool's End were growing more serious. Bill had warned me against snooping. What was he afraid I would learn? In what way was he concerned? If only I could be certain that he was on my side!

His remark accomplished one thing, though: it confirmed that there was something to be found, some hidden something to be unearthed. And as I dressed, I promised myself I would find out what that something was.

I paused in the hall downstairs, trying

to remember exactly where I had stood the night before. Yes, the wall in which I had heard the noise was one of the original walls, the thick hollow ones. Someone had been inside this wall. But where had he entered?

The answer came to me in a flash. One night I had seen someone searching McKay's office; the following night, they had been searching inside the walls. So the entrance must be in the office. And they could not search for that while I worked there, thus explaining the need to search in the middle of the night.

But how was I to search, safe from the unexpected entrance of one of the family? Any of them might come in at any time, and I could hardly lock the door to keep them out. Nor could I steal down during the night to search when I was just as likely to meet them then.

As I came into the dining room for breakfast, the answer occurred to me. Tonight was Barbara's dinner party. Sometime during the evening I was certain to find an opportunity to slip into the office and make a search of my own.

The realization that something was hidden inside the old walls, and that the doorway into those recesses was hidden somewhere close at hand, haunted me as I tried to work a little later. It was all I could do to keep from jumping up and looking at once for the hidden door. I managed to restrain myself until Jamie came down. With him there it was easier to keep from taking risks. Even so, several times I caught myself sitting staring at the walls, wondering what secrets they held.

In the middle of the morning I put another of my schemes into action. 'I'm going to be gone for a few minutes,' I told Jamie. At the door I had another thought. 'If anyone asks about me, tell them I've gone to my room for a minute,' I said.

However, I did not go to my room at all, but out of doors. I headed straight across the lawn, for the path that led to Carl's cottage. As I went, hurrying, I prayed that he would be gone, and that I would be able to talk with his wife.

Luck was with me. My knock was answered by a tiny figure of a woman, bent and wrinkled. She had a cowed manner about her as though she were frightened of the world and, remembering her husband's rude manner, I little doubted that she had reason to be. She wore a ragged skirt and a plain blouse, and she clutched a sweater about her shoulders. The sweater was a contrast to her other garments. It was of very good quality, and only a few months old, a pale blue cashmere item.

I was certain of the age of the sweater, since I had purchased it myself. It had been my going-away present to Anne.

'Hello,' I said, trying to be casual and friendly. 'I'm from up at the house. I was out for a stroll, and remembered that I hadn't yet had a chance to meet you, so . . . ' I smiled and shrugged.

'We don't get visitors much,' she said, not inviting me in. She seemed quite unsure of what to do.

'Actually, there's something I wanted to ask you about,' I said, since she hadn't bit at my first casting. 'May I come in, please?'

I thought for a moment she would refuse, but either curiosity or some inherent good manners got the best of her fear. She moved aside to let me enter.

It was a poor place, literally a cottage. This one room served as kitchen, dining and sitting room, and through an open door at the rear I saw a bedroom. The furnishings were crude, old and badly worn. The curtains were cheap and mended many times. I wondered if Carl were really so poorly paid, or if it was only that he begrudged spending any money on his home. I saw a whiskey bottle on the table, and there was another one on a shelf. I had a good idea where his money went, and I felt a wave of sympathy for the poor frightened creature before me.

'There's coffee made, if you want a cup,' she said, shyly eager to please.

'Thank you,' I said. 'I think I will, if you don't mind. Black, please.'

'We don't get much company down here,' she said as she put the cracked cup before me. I had taken a seat at the table. The coffee was weak; I wondered how far she had to stretch her grocery money, and I felt almost guilty taking the coffee.

'I'm Miss Stewart's sister,' I said. 'Anne

113

Stewart? She was here before.'

She bit her lip and said nothing, but I could see that this bit of news had increased her anxiety. I saw her glance in the direction of the door and I knew she feared the same thing I did: her husband's return.

'She left so suddenly,' I went on, determined to pursue this lead while I had the opportunity. 'I wonder if she might have mentioned her plans to you.'

She shook her head fiercely, her eyes wide circles in her withered head. 'She wasn't friendly with me, miss. I never talked to her once.'

I knew my time was running short, and I decided to be bold. 'Then how is it that you are wearing her sweater?' I demanded sharply.

She gave a little cry and jumped back as though I had struck her. 'Oh, it's no such thing,' she cried.

'It is,' I said, jumping up and seizing her trembling shoulders. 'I bought it for her myself before she came here. I ought to know it.'

She began suddenly to cry, her entire

body shaking like a leaf before a wind. I berated myself silently for being so sharp. If she became hysterical I'd never find out what I wanted to know.

'Don't cry,' I said, putting a comforting arm about the frail shoulders. 'I didn't mean to frighten you. But I'm terribly concerned about my sister. Don't you see? I must find out what has happened to her. Please, tell me how you came by the sweater.'

'I don't know nothing,' she sobbed, crying louder still and shaking her head. 'My husband gave it to me, that's all I know.'

'Then when . . . '

Before I could finish that question, the door crashed open behind me. I didn't have to look to know who was there. The terrified expression on the old woman's face told me the answer to that question.

Carl's face was livid with anger at discovering me there. 'You,' he cried. 'What are you doing here? What have you done to my wife?'

'She says the sweater belonged to the girl, that one from the house,' the woman sobbed, cringing in the face of her husband's fury.

'It *is* my sister's,' I cried.

'Get out of here!' he shouted. He came across the room, hand lifted, and I fully expected him to strike me, but at the last he regained some of his control, and instead grabbed me cruelly by the arm.

'Get out. You've got no right coming down here, snooping around, making my wife cry.'

I was half led, half dragged to the door, and before I could even voice an objection, I had been shoved outside so hard that I nearly fell on the stony ground.

'Don't come back here, not if you know what's good for you,' he said. 'If I see you hanging about here, I'll see that the missus gets rid of you for good.'

'The same way she got rid of my sister?' I demanded, too angry to be cowed. 'Or did you do that for her?'

'You're gettin' too smart for your britches,' he spat at me. 'Just remember, this is my place, and you got no right at all here.' He slammed the door in my face, so violently that the entire house seemed to shake from it.

I stood in angry frustration for a moment. I would have liked to pound on the door until he answered, and demand answers to my questions, but I knew that the effort would be futile. Inside I could hear him raging at his wife, demanding to know what she had told me. Even if he held his temper in rein so far as I was concerned, it would be taken out on that hapless creature . . . and he had barely restrained himself with me. My arm ached where he had seized it, and I was certain it would be black and blue by evening.

Dejected, I turned and started along the path toward the house.

10

For all my despondency, I could not help a feeling of excitement as the evening approached. My efforts with my dress had produced wonderful results, and I did not delude myself that I had taken such pains for any reason but to please Bill. I could hardly wait to see his admiring eyes on me when I came down for cocktails.

I took great pains with my appearance. The blue silk clung to my bosom and waist, but flared out at the hips, its fullness emphasizing every movement as I walked. I had no jewelry worthy of the costume, and so wore none, but the effect was not unpleasant. I pulled my hair back from my face and let it fall behind.

I made my way downstairs at the appointed time to join the others for cocktails in the den. It was Grant who greeted me at the door, looking elegantly handsome. Bill was nowhere in sight. I forced a smile to my lips and hid my disappointment as best I could.

'Well, our pretty little girl has blossomed into a full-fledged beauty,' Grant said, giving me a little bow. 'Will you do me the honor of letting me make the introductions?'

'Thank you,' I said, letting him take my arm. He escorted me around the group, introducing me to the guests. There was an elderly gentleman, a doctor, who remarked that they had saved the prettiest guest till last. The Henredons were a middle-aged couple who lived, apparently, nearby. Their son was a pale-faced young man who was studying medicine in San Francisco, and looked as though he would need it. There was, too, a buxom, big-voiced woman who was introduced to me as the Duchess. She had a raucous but amusing manner, and of all the people in the group, she was the one I liked best.

Barbara was there, of course, looking truly lovely in a gown of Rose Point. Bill, however, was absent.

'How about a drink?' Grant asked. He

was being charm itself, and I could not but be warm to him.

'Some sherry, I think,' I said, since it was the only thing alcoholic with which I was at all familiar. He went and returned with a glass, while the Duchess explained that her most recent husband had indeed been a duke. 'Which was his only virtue,' she informed me. 'Say, how is it a pretty little thing like you isn't married, anyway? Have the young men today all lost their eyesight?'

'No, not all of them,' a familiar voice nearby said.

I turned, and Bill was there. The admiration I had hoped for was evident in the eyes that drank me in quickly, gratefully.

My happiness was short-lived, however. He was not alone. Glenda, looking more fantastically beautiful even than I remembered, was on his arm. She wore a gown of regal purple that fitted her exquisite body like a glove. Her hair was up, like a coppery crown, and she glittered with amethysts and diamonds that womanly instinct told me were real. I felt suddenly like the country cousin, plain and shabby in my made-over dress and without a stick of jewelry.

The evening was spoiled for me. Not even the frequent glances that I got from Bill could cheer me; except for them, Glenda monopolized him completely. I was sure, too, from the glances she gave me, that she was aware of my feelings for him. She seemed actually to gloat at my discomfort.

There was nothing I could do but put the best face possible on, and pretend to be enjoying myself. I even made a pretense of flirting with Grant. It was not difficult, since he took to flirting with much the same affinity with which a duck takes to water. I could even take a certain pleasure in observing, on one occasion, that Bill seemed annoyed with the attention Grant was showering on me, but it was small recompense for the unhappiness that I was experiencing.

Mrs. Haskins had obviously gone to great pains with her cooking, and if it was short of perfection, it was certainly more impressive than what she normally served. For all that, I could scarcely enjoy it. It was with a sense of relief that I saw the last of the dishes cleared away. We lingered for a time over coffee, but I had more than one reason for cutting this time short. I wanted to do my exploring while the others were still occupied. When liqueurs were brought in, I excused myself with the pretense of a headache. It did not much comfort me to know that Bill's eyes watched me steadily as I left the room.

Once out of sight of the others, I went quickly to McKay's office. I had no idea how long my search might take, nor how much time I would have to myself. I went into the dark office, closing the door behind — and there it was again: that furtive, scurrying sound of someone moving quickly but surreptitiously. This time it was not quick enough, however; I caught him before he could dart past me.

'Jamie!' I said in surprise, holding him by the tail of his pajamas. 'You're supposed to be in bed asleep.'

He said nothing but stood looking down shamefacedly.

'You've been following me at night,' I accused him.

He looked up then, his face conscience-stricken. 'Not you — them!' he exclaimed.

'Why?'

'They've been hunting all over the place for . . . ' He paused.

'For what?' I demanded.

'Diamonds,' he said in a low voice.

'Diamonds?' I was bewildered for a moment. Anne had given me a clue in one of her letters, a clue to some exciting news she had stumbled upon. Diamonds. It had never occurred to me that there was a literal treasure hidden in the place.

'They're hidden around here somewhere,' Jamie said, as if in answer to my thoughts. 'Grandfather told me.'

I led him to the sofa and made him sit. Then I turned on one of the desk lights, low so that it would not reveal our presence outside. I sat down beside him. 'Now, I think you had better explain all this to me,' I said.

'I don't know much,' he said. Apparently gratified that he was not going to be scolded, he was warming to the spirit of adventure. 'A little while before my grandfather died, he told me that I'd be rich someday. He said Liza's diamonds would make me wealthy.'

'Liza . . . ?'

'That was my grandmother's name,' he explained. 'Only, I've never seen anything of any diamonds. So one day I asked Aunt Barbara about them. She said she didn't know anything about them, but when I told her what grandfather had said, she got all excited.'

'And since then, they've been searching the house for them,' I finished.

'But not all together,' he said. 'Sometimes Grant looks, and sometimes Aunt Barbara looks, and sometimes Bill looks.'

'But never together?'

'Aunt Barbara and Grant are together sometimes, but Bill is always by himself.'

I tried to think what that might mean. Probably, each was trying to find the treasure without the knowledge of the others. There was no honor, after all, among thieves. And I could understand now the reason for searching in the dark of night. If the diamonds had been left to

Jamie, they would not want him to know when they found them.

'Have they found them yet, do you think?' I asked aloud.

'I don't think so,' he said thoughtfully. 'That's why I came in here tonight. It's the first real chance I've had to take a look.'

I stood up, looking about the room. 'Yes, I think you're right; I think this is where they would be hidden. But just where . . . ' I paused as I glanced at him. He had the look of someone who knows more than he has told, and in a twinkling, the sense of what he had just said came to me. 'Jamie, you know, don't you? You know where they're hidden.'

He grinned and nodded. 'I think so. There's a secret place here that grandfather showed me once. If they're hidden anywhere, that must be where.'

'But where?' I asked, grinning with him. I could not help laughing to think of the time the Christians had spent searching, trying to keep their search secret from Jamie, when all the time he could have made it easier for them.

'The walls are hollow,' he said. 'When Grandfather had the house remodeled, he had to remove a lot of doors and windows and things. One of the doors was over there, where that closet is, and it came out in the hall. He covered over the opening in the hall, but on this side, he just built the closet into the space.' As he spoke, he had led the way across the room to the closet. He opened it, stepping inside. 'All you have to do is slide the back out of the way,' he said, fitting his actions to his word. The back of the closet slid aside, and there before us was a passageway. It smelled musty and damp, and was so dark that I could see little beyond the opening.

'We'll need a light,' I said.

'I've got one in my bedroom,' Jamie said.

I looked around the office. Although I hated the delay of sending him upstairs, and the risk of his being seen, there was nothing here that could be used. I gave him a reluctant nod. 'But hurry,' I said in a whisper; he was already going toward the door. 'And don't be seen.'

11

It seemed he had been gone scarcely a minute when I heard footsteps outside. They had reached the door before I realized that they were too heavy to be his.

Heart in throat, I pulled the closet door closed, just as the door from the hall opened. The darkness enveloped me. My pulse throbbed. I dared not close the sliding panel behind me for fear of the noise it might make. And if whoever was in the room now came to the closet, they would find not only me, but it as well.

In terror, I heard the steps crossing the room, coming closer to the closet! I tried frantically to think what I could say or do if I was discovered here, but nothing came to mind. There was no place to hide where I was. I had no idea what lay in the darkness beyond the opening. I could fall and break a leg trying to hide there.

I could just see the white knob in the

darkness. Whoever was outside had reached the closet door. The knob turned . . . then the hall door opened.

Jamie, I thought, with a sensation of anguish. The person with his hand on the doorknob had paused. I imagined the confrontation that must be taking place between child and adult.

But someone spoke from across the room, and it was not Jamie's voice, but Glenda's. 'Well, here you are. I was wondering what had become of you,' she said.

'Just closing things up,' Bill said from just beyond the door of the closet in which I crouched. 'I thought it looked like it might rain, and a lot of the windows are open.'

'Seems to me you've been neglecting me,' she said, coming closer. 'You've hardly spoken to me all night.'

Even in my present dilemma, I couldn't help being pleased by that bit of news.

'Sorry,' he said. 'I've had some things on my mind.'

'Like Miss Sweet Young Thing?' she asked in a catty tone that made me want to uncoil a few of those copper strands of hers.

'Toby? Yes, as a matter of fact, I have been thinking about her, but probably not the sort of thoughts you imagine.'

She must have been very close to him. Her voice sounded little more than a whisper, yet I could hear it plainly. 'Tell me,' she purred, and I could envision her claws entwined about his neck. 'Does she have my beauty?'

'No, not your beauty,' he said.

I needed no clairvoyance to interpret the silence that followed that exchange. I fought back a rush of tears and thought of Jamie. Dear Heaven, if they stayed on another minute, he would be coming in, never suspecting they were here. There was no way I could warn him without giving my own presence away.

'We'd better get back to the others,' Bill said after a minute. I heard their footsteps moving away. I began to breathe again.

'Aren't you going to finish what you were doing?' Glenda asked across the room.

'What's that?'

'You were about to do something in that closet,' she said. 'Go ahead, if you want. I'll wait.'

'No, that's all right. I was just looking for something,' he said. The door opened, and closed, and they were gone.

I had scarcely stepped from the closet, still trembling from the narrow escape, when the door opened again and Jamie slipped quickly in. I breathed a sigh. 'That was close,' I said. 'You just missed bumping into Bill and Glenda.'

'I know. They almost caught me on the stairs, but I ducked just in time.' He handed me the flashlight.

I had lost my taste for searching tonight, but I knew we might not soon have another opportunity. Taking a deep breath, I re-entered the closet. We closed the door after ourselves. 'Does this open easily from inside?' I asked, indicating the sliding panel.

'Sure,' he said, pulling it to and fro to assure me.

'Better close it then, in case anyone comes looking for us.'

We spoke in whispers. When the panel

had been closed after us, I flashed the light around. The space was narrow and low, so that I had to bend slightly to keep from bumping my head. There were open beams, old and musty, and plaster that was crumbling with age. There were exposed wires, too, where the electricity had been installed. I found myself thinking how like the image of Walter McKay I had that it was for him to have kept this secret place. Clearly, however, it was secret no more. I had given some thought to the sound I had heard in the walls the night before and concluded that it had come from in here. Now one could easily see that someone had been here recently. The dust was marked with fingerprints, footprints, handprints. Someone — one of the Christians, no doubt — had given the place a thorough going-over recently. They had found it then, at least one of them. My thoughts went back a few minutes. Bill Christian had come into the office and come straight for that closet. He must have known about the sliding panel. Perhaps he even suspected that was where I was.

131

'It looks like they've beaten us to it,' I said.

'Yeah,' he said, disappointed.

We followed the passageway to where it turned. It went only a short distance on before it ended. There were no readily discernable hiding places, and nothing lying about waiting to be discovered. It was a musty, dark corridor, completely empty.

It was a terrific let-down. I had been convinced that within these walls we would find the treasure of which McKay had hinted, and perhaps with it an answer to Anne's mysterious disappearance. Even some sort of clue would have been welcome. To find nothing was heart-breaking.

We let ourselves back into the office and, because time was fleeting and I did not want to risk being seen, we went quickly upstairs. I tried to cheer Jamie, who was even more despondent than I.

'Maybe they didn't find anything either,' I said. 'It might have been just as empty when they went in.' I sent him on his way to his room, and retired to my own.

All in all, it had been a totally unpleasant evening: Bill's interest in Glenda, my near discovery in the closet, the disappointment of the empty hiding place.

It had all been a great deal of bother, with no results to show for it.

★   ★   ★

I woke from my sleep with a start, sitting up at once. Someone had come into my room, closing the door stealthily.

'Who's there?' I demanded of the darkness, feeling for the light beside the bed.

'It's me,' Jamie whispered. 'Don't turn on the light.'

'Jamie! What is it?' I asked, clambering out of bed even as I asked.

'Come here and listen,' he said.

I came to where he was, just inside the room. He opened the door a crack. At first I heard nothing. Then, as my ears became accustomed, I made out the distant sound of low voices, just as before.

'They're still hunting,' he whispered, a jubilant note in his voice. 'That means they didn't find anything.'

I had a sobering thought. 'Or,' I said, 'one of them hasn't told the others what he found.' Nevertheless, the discovery that the search went on gave us both heart. 'We're still in the game,' I said with a grin.

'If we went . . . '

'Not tonight. It's too risky. Back to bed with you, my boy.'

He looked disappointed, but he went obediently. I watched him steal down the corridor, and returned to my own bed with renewed spirits.

★ ★ ★

Barbara was not in the dining room when I came down in the morning. I went into the kitchen to tell Mrs. Haskins that I was down, but the sound of angry voices outside the house led me in the direction of the back door.

The quarrel — and that was plainly

what it was — stopped as soon as I came into view. Both Carl and Barbara turned to glower at me.

'Mrs. Haskins had to go into town today, to shop,' Barbara snapped at me, making no pretense at pleasantries. 'You'll have to fend for yourself in the kitchen.'

'I see,' I said. Since they plainly did not care to have me hear their conversation, I went back in and found coffee on the stove. The conversation outside was continued in muted tones, and a short time later Barbara came into the kitchen.

'Carl tells me you've been down to his cottage, upsetting his wife,' she said from behind me. 'I must ask you to refrain from going there again. It is his home, after all, and he has the same right to a little privacy as anybody else, even if he is only an employee.' Her angry words conveyed the reminder that I was only an employee too.

Now that this subject had been broached, however, I was not going to be put off so easily. 'I'll be happy to stop bothering them,' I said, turning to face her, 'as soon as she will explain how she came to be in possession of my sister's sweater.'

'I think you must be mistaken,' Barbara said.

'I'm not mistaken,' I insisted. 'She was wearing an expensive sweater that belonged to my sister. Not, I am certain, a sweater that my sister would leave behind if she were going.'

'What's all the yelling about?' Bill asked, coming into the room.

'Miss Stewart has rudely accused Carl's wife of stealing one of her sister's sweaters.'

Bill cocked an eyebrow.

'I haven't said anything about stealing,' I replied, speaking to him rather than to her. How much of an ally he would be, I didn't know, but he certainly looked more sympathetic than she. 'But I do know my sister's sweater. And I want an explanation of how she came by it.'

'There's one certain way of settling this,' Bill said calmly. 'Let's go down to Carl's cottage and ask him to explain the sweater.'

'Carl's already quite furious over the

entire matter,' Barbara said.

'That's unfortunate, but I think it's best to get this straightened out right now.' He did not wait for any further discussion. 'Coming?' he asked me.

I could barely suppress a smile of triumph. 'Oh, indeed,' I assured him. Barbara came silently along, looking less pleased.

I think from the way he looked at me when we arrived, Carl would gladly have strangled me had I been alone. I was more than ever grateful for Bill's strong presence.

'Sorry to stir things up further,' Bill explained, 'but Miss Stewart seems to think your wife has a sweater of her sister's.'

'There's my wife's clothes,' Carl said angrily, indicating the closet with a sweep of his hand. 'Go snoop in them for yourself if you won't take an honest man's word.'

Bill went with me to the closet.

'It's a pale blue cashmere sweater,' I said, looking over the few items hanging there.

Of course there was nothing even remotely approaching cashmere in the closet. Bill gave me a dubious look. I turned and my eyes roamed the place. Only the dresser in the little bedroom offered any possibilities, and a quick look in its drawers revealed that there was no sweater there.

His wife had shrunk into a corner when we entered. I turned angrily upon her. 'You had it on yesterday. You must tell me where it is.'

Her eyes were wide with fright, and she shook her head so fervently I half expected it to fly off and go sailing across the room. 'You must be mistaken, miss. The only sweater I've got is this one I've got on, and you can see, it's as brown as brown can be.'

I could have slapped her, except that I could not help feeling pity for her. Heaven only knew the wrath her husband must have turned on her, and what threats forced her now to lie for his sake.

I whirled about to face Barbara. 'You were seen giving Carl a suitcase containing my sister's things,' I said, tossing my trump card on the table.

She remained unruffled, however. 'What nonsense,' she scoffed. 'How could I do a thing like that? Who told you such a silly story?'

I clenched and unclenched my fists with frustration. I could not tell the source of my information without putting Jamie in all sorts of hot water.

Barbara's face brightened, as if with inspiration. 'Oh, I do remember giving Carl a case of old clothes. They were from the house, you remember?' she turned to Bill for confirmation. 'We were going to throw them away — Grandfather's things, and even some of Grandmother's. And we thought Carl might get some use out of them.'

'I remember,' he admitted reluctantly. He turned to me. 'There's nothing here that you recognize?'

'No,' I said, fighting back hot tears. 'No, they seem to have disposed of everything.'

I ran out of the door, turning away from the house and followed the path that led into the woods. For a moment I ran blindly, thinking of nothing but being by myself for a few minutes. I ran until I came to a little clearing. The trash barrels and the wire incinerator were here. I stopped, crying into my hands. What a fool I had been!

It was some moments before I became really aware of the fire burning low in the incinerator, and a moment after that before I saw the patch of blue fabric still remaining. I stooped down, burning my hand when I put it against the hot wire.

Clothes had been burnt here. There was a lingering scent of kerosene that had helped them to burn swiftly. Probably, I thought with a bitter taste in my mouth, in the interval since I had seen Barbara and Carl quarreling. There was nothing left now but the tiny patch of blue, and even as I watched, the last of the flames licked over it. But the ashes were the ashes of fabrics, not paper; the weave could still be distinguished in some of them.

Not until I saw the faint remnants of those clothes did the full horror come to me. Anne would not have gone — not to elope, not for any reason — and left behind all of her things. My sister had never left Fool's End.

At least, not of her own volition.

12

I did not go directly back to the house. For all I knew, I would be fired and ordered from the place as soon as I did go back. In any event, I wanted time to think. So many thoughts were racing through my mind that I could not give full attention to any of them. They were a jumbled blur.

I circled the path about the house, and took the way that led down to the beach. There, seated by one of the tidal pools, I tried to make some sense of the situation in which I found myself.

That I was in danger was obvious. I should leave, I told myself, before something happened to me, as it had happened to Anne. That something had happened to Anne was no longer in question.

But one question did remain. Why had something happened to her? Simply because she had learned about the diamonds? Or had she perhaps even found them? If the latter was true, surely the family would not still be searching.

A shadow fell across the pool of water. I looked up to find Jamie standing there. 'I saw you come down this way,' he said. 'If you want to be alone, though, just say so.'

'As a matter of fact,' I said, managing a smile, 'I think I could rather use some friendly company. Pull up a rock and sit down.'

For a moment we both watched the life forms in the pool. How uncomplicated things seemed for them, I thought. Yet even as I watched, I saw a fish devour a tiny water bug.

'Jamie,' I said after a moment, 'did anything unusual happen just before my sister left?'

He thought for a moment. 'We got sick,' he said.

'Sick? Who got sick? And what kind of sick?'

'Anne and me,' he said. 'From the milk.'

My heart did a flip-flop. 'What do you

143

mean, got sick from the milk? Was it tainted, or what?'

'I don't know, exactly,' he said, speaking slowly. 'I was sick for a couple of days, and I told Anne one night when she came in to see me that my milk tasted funny. Aunt Barbara makes me drink this warm milk every night, see. Anyway, Anne tasted it and she thought it tasted funny too, kind of bitter. And that night, she got sick too.'

'Terribly sick?' I asked, a sense of dread creeping over me.

'I don't know. I didn't see her until the next day, and she looked rotten. Anyway, she asked me to do something, but to keep it a secret between us. Two things, actually. She wanted me to save her a glass of my milk, and then she wanted me not to drink any more of it until she told me to. But I wasn't to let anyone else know about it.'

I got up, feeling suddenly cold, and walked in the direction of the ocean. Jamie followed me without saying anything more. He seemed to know when I needed to think in silence.

I had overlooked the obvious. If there were something here, diamonds or any other kind of treasure, that belonged to Jamie, and the others wanted it for themselves, then Jamie was the person in danger. And if Anne had realized that, then that was how she had become endangered — why she had become a danger to the Christians. And in the same way, I would represent a threat to them.

'You think maybe it was poisoned?' Jamie asked, so abruptly that it startled me.

'No, of course not,' I said, too quickly. I looked down at him. His face showed that he did not believe me. 'Look,' I said, 'I'm going to ask the same favor as my sister. Are you still getting the milk nightly?' He nodded. 'Then bring me a glass of it tonight, if you can. And don't drink any of it.'

'I've been throwing it away,' he said. 'But I'll bring it to you tonight, after everybody's gone to bed.'

If, I thought, *I'm still here*. But I had to be, I realized with renewed determination. It was no longer a question of my own safety, or of learning what happened to Anne. Jamie was in danger, with no one here to protect him. I couldn't leave and leave him here alone with them. Whatever I had to do, whatever pride I had to swallow, I must do it in order to stay here with him, until I could think of some way of taking him away too.

I made up my mind what I must do, and when I returned to the house, I went immediately in search of Barbara. I knew that since she was angry at me, my position here was precarious to say the least. Even if Bill interceded on my behalf — and that was a highly tenuous 'if' — she seemed to be mistress here, and I could still be dismissed. With me gone, Jamie would be completely at their mercy.

Barbara was in the parlor, going over what appeared to be the family books. The look she gave me when I came in was hostile, but I met it with my humblest manner.

'I've come to apologize,' I said before she could express her anger with me. 'I'm afraid I behaved shamelessly. I don't know what more I can say than I'm sorry, and please, let me stay on and make up for it.'

I watched the various emotions chase one another across her face. She was still angry, and she still resented and disliked me, but she was a woman of strong vanity, and it had given her ego a great boost to have me humble myself before her. In the end, her vanity won out over the other feelings. 'Very well,' she said, managing a restrained smile. 'I needn't explain that I was most displeased with this morning's display. It was vulgar, at the very least.'

She paused; evidently I was expected to swallow a little more pride. I thought of Jamie and said, 'You're entirely right.'

That seemed to mollify her. 'However, we'll just forget all about it, so long as you're certain it won't happen again?' She cocked an eyebrow.

'Oh, it won't, I promise you,' I said.

'Very well. We do need the help for a while at least, and you have done well with that.'

'Thank you,' I said, nodding my head. She nodded in return, and I felt that I had been dismissed from her regal presence. I nearly backed out of the room, as was required in the presence of kings and queens, but I caught myself and left in the conventional manner.

I had gained my reprieve. I smiled grimly as I went back to the office. I had coaxed someone who was almost certainly a threat to me to allow me to remain in danger. The irony of it would have been amusing if I did not sense that the danger was so great.

13

I did not see Bill at lunch, nor did he come to the office during the afternoon. I could hardly blame him. At the very least I had made a terrific fool of myself.

Jamie came in to work with me during the afternoon, but he had scarcely arrived when Mrs. Haskins came to say that his aunt thought he ought to do some errands for her. In view of my recent conversation with Barbara I dared not intervene, and I told Jamie disconsolately that he had better do as asked.

So I was left alone. As was my custom, I quickly buried myself in my work; but as I worked, another part of my mind was busy sorting out the details of my current situation.

One thing became clear to me that had puzzled me before. Why did the Christians permit me to stay when they obviously did not want me here, and regarded me as a threat? They thought, from the clue I had given them, that Anne had discovered the diamonds for which they were searching. Despite my protestations of ignorance, they must suspect that she had passed on her information to me, or at least had given me some additional clue that would eventually lead me to them. This explained why Bill had found it necessary to steal Anne's letter from my room. They did not believe what I told them and needed to see for themselves what was in it. Perhaps they thought that the clue they needed was hidden somewhere between the lines.

This line of reasoning made me smile to myself. I had been afraid of dismissal, but so long as the Christian family thought I knew more than they, I was in no danger of being sent away.

I had another, less pleasant thought that immediately followed that one. The more the Christians thought I knew, the more of a threat I was to them — and the more danger I was in.

I had paused in my work somewhat later, and was standing at the window looking out at the view, when Grant came in. I must have looked morose, because he looked solicitous when he saw me.

'Hey, why so glum?' he asked, giving me the benefit of his most charming smile. He came to where I stood. 'A pretty afternoon, a pretty girl; I can't see anything to be glum about.'

'Sorry,' I said, trying to respond to his cheer. 'I was a thousand miles away in my thoughts.'

'Thinking about your sister?'

'Yes,' I said, meeting his gaze frankly. 'I was thinking of Anne.'

He smiled. 'You're going to feel terribly foolish when you hear from her and learn that she just went off on some lark.'

I shrugged and said off-handedly, 'Perhaps you're right.'

'Personally,' he said, putting a hand on my shoulder, 'I feel that I owe her a debt of gratitude.'

'How's that?' I asked. He was somehow closer to me. I was suddenly aware of his presence, not as a person, but as a man. I was shocked to see in his eyes something that I had not discerned there before: desire.

'If she hadn't gone, we wouldn't have had you here with us for a time.'

'And is that so important?' I asked. My mind was racing. I did not want to offend him; even his feeble support might be helpful to me. Yet . . .

His arms went about me. He drew me close, and I watched his face loom closer to mine. 'No,' I said suddenly, loudly. I turned my head, and the kiss that had been intended for my lips was delivered to my cheek instead. 'I'm sorry,' I said, disengaging myself from his arms. I was trembling with shame at how close I had come to betraying myself to a man whom I suspected of being responsible, at least in part, for my sister's disappearance.

He turned away from me, pausing to light a cigarette. He looked annoyed, although calm. It must surely have been a blow to his ego to be refused by a woman. Probably it did not happen too frequently.

'It's Bill, isn't it?' he said after a moment.

I looked full at him. 'Don't be silly,' I said, but I was nonplussed to realize that my feelings had been so transparent.

'I think it's you being silly,' he said, but without malice. He was smiling, his old charming self again. 'You must know how futile it is, your crush on my brother.'

'Even assuming that what you say is true, why would it be so futile? Perhaps you underestimate me.'

'Oh, not at all,' he assured me. 'But you see, he's going to marry Glenda.'

I willed my smile to remain in place. 'One can hardly blame him,' I said. 'She's very beautiful.'

He smiled sardonically. 'And very wealthy,' he said. 'Forgive my earlier rudeness. It was the impulse of a moment. I only thought you might welcome my embrace since you can't look forward to Bill's.'

He left the room. I bit my lip and thought of what he had told me. Yes, obviously Glenda was rich as well as beautiful. But was Bill the sort who would marry for money? I had to admit, ruefully, that I didn't really know; but if he were involved in Anne's disappearance, his character was hardly admirable.

If only I knew if I could trust him. He was not, after all, a blood relative to them. I had an almost irresistible urge to seek him out, to put myself in his hands. If it were only my own safety involved, I might take that risk, but Jamie was imperiled too, and I dared not gamble his welfare on the strength of my emotions. I had to regard Bill as guilty until proven innocent, whatever anguish it caused my heart.

Bill was at dinner, but he was more subdued than ever. I dared not think what might be the cause of it. Perhaps he was still annoyed over the embarrassing scene I had created that morning, although I had swallowed the rest of my pride and apologized to him as well. Perhaps too, he was thinking of Glenda. I took my initiative from him and ate in thoughtful silence.

Later that evening, when I was ready for bed, Jamie tapped softly at my door and came in. He had with him a jar of milk. 'I snitched the jar from the kitchen earlier,' he explained in a whisper, handing it to me.

'Good,' I said. 'Now I want you to go back to bed and forget all about this. And tonight you're not to go stealing about spying on people.'

He looked disappointed. 'Why not?' he asked.

'Because,' I said, having thought this out earlier, 'whatever the family is hunting for, they don't want us to know about it. And if they come to find out that we do know, we might be in all sorts of trouble. It will be best if we played it cool for a time.'

'But how will we know if they find the diamonds?' he asked.

'We'll just have to pray that we find them first,' I said.

'Yeah, but how will we do that if we don't have any chance to look for them?'

'Simple. If the diamonds were really here, they would surely have found them by now. So, I believe that they might be somewhere else. All we have to do is think where else they might be. Got any ideas?'

The thought that the diamonds might be somewhere other than at Fool's End was one that had come to me earlier in the day, and made a great deal of sense. The secret corridor in the walls surrounding McKay's office was the obvious place to have hidden them. If they weren't there, then it was entirely possible that they weren't in the house at all.

He thought for a moment. 'Gee, I don't know,' he said finally.

'Maybe a safe deposit box,' I suggested, thinking aloud. 'Did your grandfather do his banking locally?'

'In San Francisco, I think.' He thought for a moment more. 'Mr. Partridge would know,' he added.

'Mr. Partridge? Have I met him?'

'No. He was a lawyer in San Francisco. He was a friend of my grandfather's too. Sometimes Mr. Partridge would come here and go over a lot of things with Grandfather, and sometimes Grandfather and I would go into San Francisco. He always went to see Mr. Partridge when we were there, and sometimes he took me along.'

'Do you know the address of his office?' I asked with mounting excitement. If anyone would know about a hidden legacy, this would surely be the man.

He shook his head ruefully. 'No. But,' and his eyes brightened, 'it ought to be in Grandfather's address book, in his office desk.'

'Of course.' I stood, meaning to go for it, but at once I thought better of that. If I should encounter any of the family, I would be hard pressed to explain what I needed with an address book belonging to McKay. Morning would be soon enough to look for it.

'That's the first place we'll look,' I said, considerably cheered. 'And now, off to bed with you, young man.' I walked with him to the door. There I paused to ask, 'Do you know anything about Glenda?'

'Like what?'

'Like have you heard anything about her and Bill?'

He shrugged as if the information could be of little consequence. 'Just that Aunt Barbara says they're going to get married. Why?'

'Nothing,' I said. 'All right, off with

you. And remember, stay in bed when you get there.'

I saw him out, and watched until he had made his way down the hall. Then I closed my door quietly, and went to my own bed. My spirits had fallen considerably.

14

The next morning at breakfast, I prepared the way for a trip to San Francisco. 'I wonder if anyone would mind my taking a day off,' I said to Barbara. 'I hadn't really planned on staying over here, and there are a number of things I need to pick up.'

'When were you planning on going?' Bill asked.

'There's no real hurry,' I said. Of course I was eager to go as quickly as possible, but I did not want to rouse any suspicions by seeming eager. 'Tomorrow, or the day after.'

'Tell you what,' Bill said. 'Make it the day after, and I'll drive you in. I have a few errands I ought to see to myself.'

'I don't see why that's necessary,' Barbara said, looking displeased. 'The bus stops right down at the road and the service is quite good.'

'That's right,' I agreed quickly. 'It's silly

for you to put yourself out.'

'No trouble,' he assured me, giving me a smile that was certain to end any resistance I might have. 'I have to make the trip anyway, and I can't think of any better company to have.'

'Thank you,' I said, blushing like a schoolgirl. 'Day after tomorrow, then.'

It was not a long delay, and another idea had occurred to me. With the trip into the city, and away from Fool's End, I might be able to pry some information out of Bill. Of course, I did not admit to myself the other reason — perhaps the major one — for accepting his offer. However, I did not mean to waste the two days in between, either. The nearest town was not quite five miles away. I did not want to confuse my alibis by mentioning shopping again, but I had already seen that the garage contained a pair of bicycles, and I was certain that no one would object to my going for a ride. During the morning I asked Jamie if he could ride.

'Sure,' he said, looking a bit taken aback that I should even have found it necessary to ask.

'Think town and back is too far for an afternoon spin?' I asked.

'Not for me,' he replied, with a faint suggestion in his voice that it might be too far for me.

At lunch, I asked if Jamie and I couldn't go for a ride during the afternoon. 'I don't think he gets all the exercise he should,' I added, addressing myself to the men, whom I thought would be more sympathetic. 'And neither do I, these days. I'll go to rack and ruin pretty soon.'

'I wouldn't worry too much about that,' Grant said with his usual flirtatious smile.

'You're right, it would probably be good for him,' Bill said. 'Better not go too far, though.'

'Any particular destination in mind?' Grant asked.

I avoided meeting his eyes. 'Oh, I thought we'd just follow the wind,' I said, hoping that the wind blew in the direction of the village.

Soon after lunch, when I had switched

to a full skirt, Jamie and I set out. It was a lovely day, clear and crisp, so that our ride seemed perfectly reasonable. He had not questioned our purpose in going, and I did not want to worry him unduly with my own fears.

He was knowledgeable about the terrain, and I found him a good guide. He knew most of the trees, and identified a number of flowers and other plants. His quick eyes spotted birds that I would have missed.

Although I was used to bicycling, the terrain was mostly up and down, and I was grateful when at last we saw the roofs of the little town. There wasn't much to it. We came in on the main street that led straight through, with little unpaved streets branching off of it. The center of town was an intersection of ours and another road. About the intersection were clustered the town's business establishments: a service station, a market, general store, a drug store, and a town hall, which housed the police and fire departments as well.

It needed no great amount of coaxing

to sell Jamie on the idea of a soda. 'Aren't you having one too?' he asked when I ordered for him.

'In a little while,' I said. 'I have an errand to run first. Do you happen to know where the local doctor's office is, by the way?'

'White house on the last corner back; we passed it coming in,' he said. 'Why?'

I smiled and messed his hair. 'Drink slowly,' I said, putting a dollar on the table. 'I'll be back in a couple of minutes.'

The doctor's waiting room, actually the front room of his house, was empty. A little bell sounded as I came in, to alert him to my presence. In a minute a door to the inner office opened and a plump little elf of a man appeared before me.

'Doctor Moore?' I greeted him; he nodded. 'I'm Miss Stewart, from Fool's End. I wonder if I might have a minute of your time?'

'Yes, yes, surely,' he said, cheerful and enthusiastic. He ushered me into the inner room. 'Have a chair, Miss Stewart.' He indicated a seat beside the battered oak desk. He scratched a spot on his head that had long since seen the last of its hair. 'Miss Stewart? Seems like the other girl up there was a Stewart, wasn't she?'

My pulse quickened. 'Yes, that was Anne, my sister. Did you know her?'

'No, only by sight. Met her once or twice when I was up to the house.'

'Then you know the Christians,' I said. I opened the large carry-all purse I had with me. In it was the jar of milk Jamie had brought me. I knew little about such matters, but I was certain that a doctor would be able to analyze it, or know where to have that done.

'Oh, yes,' he said, beaming. 'Known them for years, even before my sister went up there to work.'

My mouth fell open. 'Your sister?' I echoed.

He nodded, apparently proud of the connection. 'Myrtle,' he said. 'Name's Haskins now. Why, what's this? Milk?'

It was too late to hide the jar. My hand shaking, I put it on his desk and pretended to search in my purse for something else, while my brain raced. 'Yes,' I said aloud, 'I came in on a bicycle.

I thought I might get thirsty.'

'Must be warm by now,' he said, reaching for it. 'Let me get you some fresh. I'll just pour this into mine.'

'No.' I reached for it so abruptly that the inevitable happened. It slipped from my nervous fingers and crashed to the floor. Glass and milk splashed across the room.

'How stupid of me,' I cried, jumping to my feet.

The doctor was kindness itself. 'No matter,' he said. 'I'll have my wife clean it up, don't you trouble yourself over it at all.' He went to another door that led deeper into the recesses of the house. 'Helen,' he yelled, 'had a little accident in here. Better bring a broom and a mop.'

He closed the door and turned back to me. 'Now, maybe we'd better go in here in the examining room, while she cleans that up.'

I was still shaking, but the moment's respite had let me think of an excuse for my visit. 'I had a prescription that needs refilling,' I said, digging into my purse again. 'And since it's from out of town, I thought it might be best to have you write a new one. But I seem to have left the empty bottle at home.'

'What was it for?' he asked, assuming a more business-like manner.

'Sleeping pills,' I said, still digging through the purse's contents for the nonexistent bottle.

'Umm, I see,' he said, frowning. 'Don't like to prescribe that sort of thing without a full examination, you know. Course if you had brought the bottle . . . ' he let the sentence trail off and watched my search.

I made a gesture of futility and sighed. 'Well, I seem to have left it at home. Looks like I wasted a trip. You're sure you wouldn't . . . '

He shook his head solemnly. 'Don't like to do that. Not always the best thing, don't you see.'

I sighed again and smiled resignedly. 'Yes, I suppose it's wisest.' I stood. 'I am sorry about that accident. How much do I owe you for the call?'

'Not a cent,' he said, standing too. 'I didn't do a thing for you, anyway.'

We went out through the first office. A

frail woman in a somber gray dress, her hair plaited about her head, was just finishing cleaning up the milk and broken glass. She looked at me with frank curiosity.

'Well, thank you again,' I said at the other door. 'If I'm coming in again, I'll bring it then.'

'You do that,' he said. 'Goodbye now. Say hello to my sister.'

I promised I would, and went out to the street, where I breathed a sigh of relief. I had come within a fraction of a second of asking the kindly old gentleman for his aid. It would almost certainly have gotten back to Fool's End, probably sooner than I did. I ought to have realized that it would be unsafe to make inquiries here, where the Christians were so close and so well known. Whatever I wanted to find out, I would have to do my checking when I got to San Francisco. There was no telling who in town might be related to whom. For all I knew, the druggist, who had been my other hopeful source of information, might be related to the Christians themselves.

Jamie gave me an inquisitive look when I came up to his table at the drugstore. 'The doctor says it's my nerves,' I said, thinking that would settle his curiosity regarding my visit to the doctor. 'Think you could drink another of those sodas?'

He thought he could; I ordered one for each of us. We drank them in silence broken only by an occasional remark. When we had finished, I made a point of buying a few articles — some cologne, a box of tissues — as an additional excuse for the trip, just in case the story of our visit did get back to Fool's End.

It was already mid-afternoon when we started out of town. We talked little as we rode; the trip back was mostly uphill, and I for one needed most of my breath to keep up with Jamie's energetic pace. Nor did I try to slow him down. I was afraid that if we were too late in arriving back, future trips out might be more difficult.

Somewhere behind us the sound of a car's engine broke the silence of the woods. It contrasted with the scolding of a jay somewhere overhead. I was only vaguely aware of the car's sound as it came nearer, climbing the road behind us.

When I realized that it was coming our way, I dropped behind Jamie, so that we were in a single file. 'Better stay off on the shoulder,' I warned. He nodded and veered to the right, onto the narrow strip of gravel.

The car was coming fast. I heard its tires squeal in protest as a curve was taken too fast. It sounded as if the car skidded.

A sense of danger engulfed me. I swerved sharply to the right, well onto the grass, and stopped. 'Jamie,' I called, meaning to tell him to do the same, but the car took the corner behind us then, and my voice was lost in the roar of the engine and the screaming of the tires on the pavement.

Jamie looked back over his shoulder. The gesture was enough to make him veer onto the edge of the road. The car hurtled by me, a flash of red, skidding violently.

Even before the scream could form in my throat, the car had struck the boy on the bicycle.

15

I screamed as the frail young body hurtled across the roadway, thrown from the bike. The car careened out of control for a moment, coming to a halt finally yards up the road. By then I was off my bike and running toward the still figure in the grass.

He lay motionless, eyes closed. There was blood running across his forehead. I bent, grabbing his wrist to feel for a pulse. It was there, but faint.

Someone was running. In my anxiety for the boy, I had virtually forgotten the car and the careless driver that had struck him. I looked up, furious at what they had done; but the angry words stuck in my mouth. The person running toward me was Bill Christian.

'Good grief,' he said, running up. 'Is he . . . ?'

'He's unconscious,' I said, unable to contemplate the significance of the accident. 'I can't tell how badly he's hurt.'

Someone else was coming from the direction of the car. It was Glenda. She looked little more than mildly concerned. There was an arrogant chip on her shoulder that seemed to defy anyone to make an issue of what had happened. I was more than ready to knock it off, however.

'Who was driving?' I demanded, looking from one to the other.

Bill was examining Jamie and did not look up. Glenda gave me a frosty look. 'I was,' she said coldly. 'The car got away from me on the corner. When I saw you two, right in our way, I tried to stop, and the car went out of control. It was your fault, you know.'

I was so angry I was nearly spitting. 'That's a lie,' I cried. 'We were well out of your way. If you hadn't been driving like a lunatic . . . '

'Standing here trading accusations isn't going to do Jamie any good,' Bill cut into our argument. He looked at me. 'Will you ride down to town for Doctor Moore while we take him up to the house?'

'No,' I said firmly. I had no intention of entrusting him to their care. 'I won't leave him.'

'Well I can't ride a bicycle,' Glenda announced haughtily. 'I never had to learn.'

Bill looked as though he might slap both of us, but he seemed to realize that I did not mean to be persuaded. 'Looks like I'll have to go, then, and you two will have to take him to the house.'

I little cared for the idea of riding with her, but it seemed the lesser of the evils. I helped Bill put him into the diminutive rear seat of the car. He removed his jacket and put it over the inert form, then moved back to let me get into the passenger's seat.

'You'd better warn her to drive slowly,' I said.

'I'm quite an accomplished driver,' she snapped.

'I just had a demonstration of your abilities,' I replied just as sharply. 'And in case you're not familiar with the law, if he dies, you'll be guilty of manslaughter.'

The threat seemed to take some of the wind out of her sails. Her mouth snapped shut in a straight, angry line. She slammed the door shut on her side.

'I'll be up with Doctor Moore as fast as I can,' Bill said, closing my door gently but firmly. 'Have Grant put him into bed for you.' Then he was gone, running for the bicycle. He was on it and riding downhill even before we had started off.

Notwithstanding her anger, Glenda drove slowly and cautiously, almost pointedly slowly in fact. I did not object. A minute or two more in getting there would probably not make a great deal of difference. The sharp jolts of a rough ride might.

When we were near the house, I leaned across and began to blow the horn loudly and insistently. By the time we pulled up to the house, both Grant and Barbara had come to investigate the racket.

'Bring him inside,' I told a startled Grant. If he objected to my ordering him about, he did not show it. He carried Jamie quickly inside and up to his room.

Bill was there quickly indeed. We had not been far out of town and he must have ridden like a demon. By the time we had Jamie comfortably ensconced in his bed, Bill and Doctor Moore were pulling into the drive.

I remained in the room while the doctor examined him. I did not know a great deal about nursing, but I wanted an accurate report, from the horse's mouth as it were, of how Jamie was.

As it turned out, he was not so badly off as he might have been. 'A pretty lucky boy, I'd say,' Doctor Moore concluded. 'The car must have just brushed him. There are a lot of bruises and scrapes, and a nasty cut over one eye. A mild concussion. But otherwise, he's all right. Nothing broken, no internal injuries that I can detect.' He pulled a sheet over the still unconscious form, and turned to me again. 'How did this happen, exactly?'

I told him briefly my version of the incident. He scowled as he listened.

'I think there ought to be charges of some sort brought,' I finished. I was still angry, and frightened, at what had been a narrow escape. I was even more frightened by what I hadn't told him: my fears that perhaps it had not been an accident. How closely Glenda was involved with the family I did not know, but I was not dismissing the possibility that the accident had been engineered.

'Yes, I see,' the doctor said. After a moment's thought he added, 'This is a small town, don't you know; things aren't always done here the way they would be elsewhere.'

'Are you suggesting nothing should be done?' I asked. 'That boy was almost killed by a driver's criminal negligence.'

'I think perhaps I ought to talk to the Christians,' he said.

'But they weren't there, except for Bill,' I argued. 'What difference can it make what Grant or Barbara have to say?'

'I think I'll talk to them just the same,' he said, giving me a frosty look. He left me, finding his own way downstairs. He had scarcely gone when Bill came out of his room and into the one in which Jamie was lying.

'How is he?' he asked in an anxious voice.

'He'll be all right,' I said sharply. 'No thanks to you.'

He winced visibly. 'It was my fault,' he said. 'We were quarreling. She drives like a madwoman when she's angry. I'd never have forgiven myself if . . . ' he let the sentence go unfinished. 'Where is the doctor?'

'Downstairs, with Barbara and Grant. Unless I'm mistaken, they're arranging to whitewash the entire incident.'

'Yes, they'll do that,' he admitted sadly. He looked up at me. 'There's nothing we can do about it, either. Even if I went into town and reported it all to the sheriff, he would simply come up himself and talk to them, and it would still be whitewashed.'

Some of my anger faded as I began to realize how truly sorry Bill was for what had occurred. I had an urge to reach out to him, to comfort him, but I held back. I could still not take the risk of trusting him, especially not after this incident. It was entirely possible that it had been an accident, but there was also the possibility that it had been something more ominous. My fears for Jamie's safety were greatly increased. More than ever, I had to face this challenge on my own, trusting no one.

I postponed my trip to San Francisco. Much as I wanted to learn the answers to the questions that troubled me, I dared not risk leaving Jamie in his present condition. I remained with him for the next two days. On the third day, Doctor Moore permitted him to get out of bed, and by the fourth day he seemed completely recovered.

During this time, two things struck me as significant. Barbara came to me once to offer a favor. 'I have to go into town,' she explained sweetly. 'I thought I'd fill that prescription for you.'

'What prescription?' I asked. I had been reading, and the significance of her remark did not fully strike me.

'The one you went into town to have filled the day of the accident,' she explained.

In the excitement over the accident I had nearly forgotten the original purpose of our trip, and that it had been taken somewhat surreptitiously.

'I won't need it, it seems,' I said. 'I've had no trouble sleeping lately.'

It was lame, I knew. I did not think she really believed in the prescription, or wanted to have it filled for me. I felt that she only wanted to tell me she knew of our trip and where we had gone.

I could only suppose that the doctor had told her of the spilt milk, too. Whether she had guessed the meaning behind that, I could not tell, but the second happening of significance during this period was that Jamie's evening milk came to a halt. It was a relief, in a sense, and a disappointment in another. Now I would never know if it had been harmless, or in some way poisoned.

★ ★ ★

I neglected my work during the period of Jamie's convalescence. No one seemed to mind, or even to notice. I little cared if they did. I was determined to remain with Jamie as much as possible until he was

178

well over the effects of his accident. He was in danger enough under the best of circumstances; I wanted no one to take advantage of his incapacity.

In fact, after a few days, the incapacity was nothing more than some stiffness and soreness. Soon after he was out of bed we began to take walks. It gave us time out of the house to ourselves, and gave him some exercise and fresh air.

It also very nearly cost us our lives.

We had gone out one noon for a walk. Sometimes we went into the woods and sometimes, as Jamie got better, we went to the beach. This day we went to the beach and, because he felt particularly frisky, we went further than was usual on our walks.

When the rain began, we were quite a long distance from home. It came up so swiftly that we were inescapably caught in it. By the time we recognized the clouds and started back in the direction of Fool's End, it had already started to rain.

'Looks like we'll have to run for it,' I said, looking vainly about for some place to sit it out, but there was nothing around

179

that offered any sort of shelter.

By the time we reached the path that led up to the house, it was pouring, and we were both drenched. I called myself every sort of fool for not having paid more attention to the weather. I could imagine what Barbara would have to say about my negligence.

The path was muddy and slippery, and we had to move with caution, Jamie leading the way as usual. It was the perilous condition of the path, however, that saved our lives.

We were near the top, on a narrow strip of a ledge, when my foot slipped. I nearly lost my balance, grabbing at a root in the side of the cliff, and giving a little cry. Jamie stopped at once, looking back.

At the same instant, I caught a suggestion of movement above, just out of the corner of my eye. 'Look out,' I cried. Jamie jumped toward me, and the huge rock that had come crashing and sliding down the slope shot past him, bounced off the ledge, and disappeared below.

We stood in horrified silence for a moment, staring with wide eyes at one another. I looked up. The instant before the rock fell, I thought I had seen someone, the figure of a man. It had vanished now — if it had even been there. It had been too quick, too unexpected.

I shivered and moved to put an arm about Jamie. He was trembling. Surely someone had not deliberately pushed that rock. Had I not slipped, it would have struck us, thrown us over the ledge to our deaths.

Another accident, or . . . ?

We finished the trip back to the house with extreme care. Mrs. Haskins looked dismayed when we splashed into her kitchen, both of us dripping wet. 'I wonder if you'd be so good as to fix us some hot tea,' I said to her as we passed. 'I think we'll need it.'

She nodded, and we went on. In Jamie's room I instructed him to get out of his wet clothes at once and into a warm bath. There were accidents enough plaguing him; I did not want pneumonia on top of them.

By the time I had changed into dry clothes, Mrs. Haskins had brought the tea. 'You ought to have a hot bath, if you'll pardon my saying so,' she said.

'In a moment,' I said, putting a sweater about my shoulders. 'Take Jamie some tea, too. Tell him I'll be along in a little while.'

I meant to make a full report to the family of the latest accident; but more to the point, I wanted to know if any of them had been out in the rain.

I had the answer to that before I even got downstairs. I met Bill on the stairs. He was soaked to the skin. My own hair, of course, was still wet, so that he could easily enough see where I had been. 'Looks like we both got caught,' he said with a grin.

I did not return the smile. I was not feeling particularly amused. 'We were out for a walk,' I said. 'How did it happen you got caught?'

'I was looking for you,' he said. When I made no reply to that, he went on, 'I thought I'd enjoy having a stroll with you, so I came to look for the two of you. No luck, though. All I found was the rain.'

'You came toward the beach?' I asked.

'Good Lord, no. Was that where you were? I went into the woods.' When he saw that I still was angry, he asked, 'Why?'

'We had more than a little rain to discomfort us,' I explained. I told him briefly about the falling rock. I did not add that there might have been someone above us who might have caused the rock to fall.

He seemed, however, genuinely concerned about the accident. 'Lord,' he said, running a hand through his wet hair. 'There's some sort of black cloud hanging around, isn't there?'

'If you believe in black clouds,' I said. I left him there, looking after me, and went on my way downstairs. I found no one in the downstairs of the house, or none of the family at any rate. Barbara, Mrs. Haskins informed me when I asked, had been in her room since before the rain started. It seemed she had a headache. And Mr. Grant was out, Haskins knew not where.

I went back upstairs to Jamie's room and drank some hot tea. He seemed, all in all, not too badly off. I could see that this accident, so close on the heels of the other, had unnerved him, but he had a streak of stoicism in him that kept him steady. I could not but reflect that he would be a fine man when he grew up. If, I thought morbidly, he managed to grow up.

When the rain had stopped, I decided to go on an errand. I followed the path about the house, toward the cliff. It was not difficult to find the spot from which the rock had fallen. I had hoped that I might also find something in the way of tracks that would give me a clue as to how it had fallen, but the rain had washed away any evidence, if indeed any had ever existed. There was nothing to show that the rock had not fallen from the most natural of causes.

I went back to the house and took a warm bath. It was time, I decided, that I went to San Francisco. Nor did I intend to leave Jamie here, in the path of any further accidents. I meant to take him with me, whatever arguments I had to use to convince his family.

16

I was surprised that I had no difficulty in arranging for Jamie to travel with me. I sensed Barbara's disapproval as soon as I broached the subject, which I did the same evening at dinner, but Bill intervened before she had an opportunity to voice her objections.

'I think it's a great idea,' he said at once. 'He hasn't been away from this house since his grandfather passed on.'

'Why should he want to go anywhere? Fool's End is a lovely place,' Barbara said.

'Lovely, and gloomy, and dull,' he pointed out. 'It's settled, then. The three of us will make a real holiday of it.'

Neither Grant nor Barbara looked pleased with the idea, but Jamie's enthusiasm more than made up for their lack of it. For myself, I felt more a sense of relief than any excitement. True, accidents had happened to him already while I was around, but I felt I had at least a fighting chance to keep him safe if he were with me. Heaven alone knew what other accidents might occur if I left him behind.

We left early in the morning. It was a good morning's drive, through scenic mountains and forests, following the coast. I had never been through this area, and I gave the passing views my rapt attention.

Jamie was literally a bundle of excitement, carrying on a running stream of chatter. Bill had apparently left behind at Fool's End the somber manner that he usually wore there, and was only slightly less boyish than Jamie. The two of them pointed out things of interest. We joked and laughed a great deal. I was more relaxed than I had been since my arrival at Fool's End. I was truly sorry when, in time for a late lunch, we arrived at San Francisco. We swept down into that most beautiful of all cities, across a breathtaking bridge; and there all about us was the charm and commotion, the loveliness of the 'city by the bay', as I had heard the locals dubbed it.

Bill had booked rooms for us at the Fairmount, one of the city's most elegant hotels. I was overwhelmed by the marble and gilt of that splendid lobby, so much more impressive than any modern composition of glass and steel could ever be. We had no sooner checked in and had lunch, than Jamie was ready to take in the sights. And although I had not come for the purpose of sightseeing, I was nearly as eager as he to do so. Nor was Bill reluctant.

'No use taking the car,' he said, taking charge of our expedition. 'This is a city to see on foot, and from cable cars.'

That was how the afternoon was spent: on foot, and in cable cars. We rode the clanging, colorful little vehicles up and down hills that seemed only a little less than perpendicular. We saw the garage from which the cable cars rode out. We saw Chinatown and strolled up and down narrow, mysterious-looking streets.

We went to Fisherman's Wharf. It was a cacophony of sounds, melodious in their very disharmony. By this time we had worked up an appetite, which we satisfied with little shrimps from a vendor's stall. Out in the bay was the island that had once kept men imprisoned.

It was nearly sundown when we arrived back at the hotel. Jamie showed evidence of being tired, despite his protestations that he wasn't. I myself felt the desire to kick off my shoes for a while.

'Just don't get too comfortable,' Bill warned me. 'Dinner is at eight. As for you, young man, you get dinner in your room, and an evening of television. I have plans for your governess.' He gave Jamie a wink and, to my surprise, rather than being put out at being set aside, Jamie seemed happy to let us go our ways. I did not learn until later that he had been promised a generous reward for co-operating in Bill's plans for the evening.

I hadn't expected a night on the town, and in fact I was unprepared for one, but before we had left Fool's End, Barbara had surprised me by paying me the salary I had coming for the work I had done. I took one look at the sorry wardrobe I had with me, and called to ask the switch-board operator to suggest a place to find a nice dress for the evening.

Bill knocked at my door at eight. By that time I was poorer by nearly all of the salary I had earned, but dressed to the teeth. I had gone for a midi, a wool knit in black the price of which gave me little shivers. There had been enough left for a strand of cultured pearls, a diminutive bag, and a pair of shoes in which I nearly had to learn to walk all over again.

Perhaps it was clairvoyance on his part, but Bill had a package with him which he handed me as soon as I opened the door. 'I forgot to warn you about the cold nights here,' he said. 'So I went back out for this. It was my mother's. Since she died, it's done nothing but gather dust in storage here.'

It was the very thing I had joked with the salesgirl about as I bought the dress. 'This dress is just longing for fur,' I told her with a laugh. 'And it's going to get nothing but an old wool sweater.'

Now here was the fur I had dreamed

of, without ever believing it would come true. I was almost afraid to touch it. When I did, I knew that I had never felt anything so soft.

'It's sable,' he said. 'Put it on.'

I shook my head. 'I don't think I should. It's too expensive. And not the sort of thing a girl ought to accept from a man.'

He smiled. 'You don't have to accept it permanently. As I said, it's my mother's, and supposedly for the girl I marry. But there surely can't be anything compromising in borrowing it for the evening, can there?'

'I suppose not,' I agreed.

'Well, then,' he said. He took it from the package and put it about my shoulders. I would have liked to have worn it forever; I would have liked to have been the girl who was entitled to keep it, by virtue of marriage. Even if I never had that honor, however, I could enjoy one evening of elegance.

We dined at a delightful little place atop a hill. The building had once housed smugglers, so we were told. I suppose the food was good. Everything tasted of stardust to me.

From there we went to a discotheque with music loud enough to shatter everything but my mood. And after that there was a theater club with a satirical revue, *Beach Blanket Babylon*, that kept us both laughing boisterously. Bill held my hand throughout the show.

Later — I refused to let myself wonder how late it really was — we went to a quieter spot, an intimate club with more romantic music and dancing. We had brandy Alexanders, which Bill had to warn me to take slowly. 'They taste harmless, but they aren't,' he explained.

Of course I was already drunk on the night, the music, and his wonderful presence. He was charm itself. This was a side to his personality that I had only glimpsed before. I was surprised when he said very nearly the same thing about me.

'You ought to let yourself go like this more often,' he said. 'You have no idea how lovely you are tonight. Not,' he added quickly, 'that you aren't always lovely. You are, of course. But tonight you're breath-taking.'

'You could turn a girl's head,' I said with a happy laugh.

'I wish I could turn yours,' he said. 'I wish I could make it spin.'

'Doesn't Glenda's do enough spinning for you?' I asked. I was sorry as soon as the words were out of my mouth. A frown crossed his face like a cloud. 'I'm sorry,' I said at once, 'I didn't mean that to sound as catty as it did.'

He looked somewhat abashed, but frank. 'As a matter of fact, I guess if I'm going to woo you with sweet phrases, you have every right to bring her up.'

'No, I haven't,' I protested. 'It's none of my business whom you marry.'

'But it is,' he argued. 'At least, you have a right to know I have no intention of marrying Glenda.'

'But . . . I thought you were engaged. And she's so very beautiful.'

'And you're not, I suppose?' he said with some amusement.

'I'm not crazy enough to think I look like that.'

'No, you're right,' he said, 'you don't

look like that at all.' He signaled for the waiter, who was standing nearby. The man came at once to see what we wanted.

'Tell the young lady what she looks like,' Bill said. 'She has some sort of notion in her head that she's not pretty,' Bill explained, while I suffered an agony of embarrassment. 'I just wondered what you thought about it.'

He smiled widely then. 'I think she's very much mistaken,' he said. 'She is the loveliest woman in the place.'

'Thank you,' Bill said, dismissing him. 'Satisfied?' he said to me.

'Embarrassed to death,' I replied, although of course I was flattered out of my wits as well.

'Anyway,' Bill went on, 'the point really is, Glenda means nothing to me. Barbara and Grant have done everything but lock us in a dungeon together, trying to promote a romance, but it just isn't there — not on my side, anyway. That's what she was so angry about the other day. I told her I couldn't marry her because I was in love with . . . with someone else.'

I wished that I could have the courage

to ask who that 'someone else' was, but I didn't. And he didn't volunteer the information. Instead, he signaled for the waiter again, and asked for our check.

'Time to get you home to bed, Cinderella,' he said, helping me from my chair.

At the door to my room, Bill took my key to unlock my door for me, but he barred the way so that I could not go in at once.

'I've been trying to get up the nerve to tell you something all evening,' he said. 'It's a little difficult. But if I don't say it now I may never say it.' He paused. Then, speaking more quickly, he went on. 'That day you came to Fool's End, I was looking out the window and saw you walking up to the house. I fell in love with you, literally at first sight. I've loved you ever since.'

I could say nothing. I could only stand and stare. Luckily he seemed to expect no answer. He took me quickly in his arms and kissed me, briefly and tenderly. Then he opened my door and left me.

17

I woke with a smile of joy on my lips. As sleep faded, however, so did my smile.

I sat up, frowning at my own image in the mirror on the wall. I could not on one hand insist to myself that I loved him and that he loved me, and on the other hand suspect him of having done away with my sister, and of trying to do away with Jamie and with me.

And though I suffered agony because of it, I could not take the chance, which my heart cried out to me to take, of trusting him completely. If it were only my own safety involved, I would gladly have taken the risk, but I had no right to throw away Jamie's safety on the strength of my romantic impulses.

As if he had heard my thoughts, Jamie knocked at the door connecting his room with mine, and at my bidding, came in.

'Hi,' he said. 'Gonna sleep all day?'

I tossed a pillow at him. 'How about

ordering some coffee?' I said, 'while I make myself presentable.'

We had coffee and rolls. Bill called to see what our plans were. 'I have plans for the afternoon,' I said. 'But I know a young man who would probably enjoy an outing, if you have one in mind.'

'Great. Tell him to put himself together and scoot over here.'

When Jamie had gone, I called Amos Partridge, Walter McKay's attorney friend. I had brought the number with me from Fool's End. Mr. Partridge, his receptionist told me, was very busy. I explained that I was a friend of the family and wanted to talk to him about the McKay estate, and that I was only in town for the day. The McKay name apparently still carried weight, because a moment later the girl informed me that Mr. Partridge would see me at one.

I was there promptly. A slim, pale girl ushered me into Mr. Partridge's office. He rose to greet me as I came in. 'Miss Stewart?' he said. 'I'm Amos Partridge. I understand you were a friend of McKay's.'

He was a wizened old man, in his seventies at least, although quite spry. He had a look of helpless innocence in his face, except for his eyes. They were wary and sharp, and revealed a certain cunning. I guessed that it would be hard to deceive this man. Nor did I mean to. I had made up my mind in advance to tell him the truth, laying my cards on the table as it were, and to trust in his professional discretion.

'Actually, no,' I admitted, having the seat he offered. 'I'm a friend of his grandson's.'

'Jamie?' The quick look that crossed his face revealed more surely than words that he felt a genuine affection for the boy. 'Haven't seen him for a while. Is he in town with you?'

'Yes. I would have brought him with me, except that I wanted to be free to talk quite bluntly with you. May I, please?'

'By all means,' he assured me, taking a seat behind his desk.

I began with my arrival at Fool's End, and told of Anne's disappearance, and of the accidents that had been occurring. I did not mention the diamonds, yet; I hoped perhaps he might bring them up himself, if they existed. They were, I knew, the most melodramatic part of my story, and I wanted it to sound as credible as possible.

He let me tell my story without interruptions, watching me closely the whole time. It was impossible to tell what he was thinking, or how he was taking it.

'I know I'm asking you to accept a great deal,' I concluded. 'After all, I'm a stranger to you, while you have known these people for some time. And it is hard to believe that anyone should want to harm a young boy like Jamie.'

'Stranger things have happened,' he said, reaching for his pipe. 'Do you mind if I smoke?' I assured him I did not, and for a moment he occupied himself with filling and lighting the pipe. When he had it going to his satisfaction, he spoke again. 'The only real drawback is that the family has no motive for harming the boy, you see.'

'I thought perhaps it was something to do with the will,' I said, feeling a little disappointed that he remained unconvinced.

He chuckled and took a deep puff on the pipe. 'The estate isn't very large, you know. And what there is of it, for the most part, went into a trust for Jamie, until his twenty-first birthday. That applied to the house as well as the monies and such. There's a distant cousin in Los Angeles who got a small amount of cash. The rest, which I'm afraid was modest, went to Mrs. Christian, her son Grant, and William. William isn't really related, you know, except that his father married Mrs. Christian after she divorced her first husband. But McKay was fond of him and left him a little too. That's about all there was. The will stipulated that the Christians had to look after Jamie until he is of age.'

'But wouldn't they profit if he died before then?' I argued. 'They'd get all that money.'

He shook his head. 'In the first place, as I said, there wasn't a great deal. In the second place, they wouldn't get it anyway. If Jamie should die before reaching twenty-one, the trust does not revert to the family but is to be used as a fellowship fund for beginning writers.' He paused; then, remembering something else, he added, 'There are some exceptions, but not of real consequence. A few personal items went directly to the boy. I suppose they would become the relatives' property if anything happened to him. Personal papers, some clothing, a few pieces of inexpensive jewelry — nothing of value there, I can assure you.'

'But wouldn't the personal papers be of some value?'

'I doubt it. He'd already published two volumes of those in his later years. I doubt that there's much left but some miscellaneous scraps, and the carbons of his earlier works.'

He was right, of course. I had been working on those papers myself, and it was doubtful if the entire lot would produce enough for a book. The mention of jewelry, however, had brought me back to the one piece of information I hadn't yet imparted to him, and I felt that I had to do so now to convince him.

'You mentioned that McKay's jewelry goes directly to Jamie,' I said. 'I have reason to believe that there is more of that than a few insignificant pieces.'

His eyebrows lifted. 'How is that?' he asked.

I told him of the references to Liza's diamonds, which McKay had told his grandson would make him wealthy. To my surprise, this did not have the effect I had expected of convincing him. He stood, putting his hands behind his back, and walked to the window, looking out for a moment.

'I'm afraid that, too, is but an illusion,' he said at last, turning back to me. 'Do you know the story of Liza and her diamonds?' I shook my head. 'Liza was his wife, of course — Jamie's grandmother. An exquisitely beautiful woman when I met her, and she was no longer young then. I can scarcely imagine what she must have looked like when she was young. Certainly it was enough to catch McKay's tough old heart. He fell in love with her at first sight — so he always said — and from the way they acted toward one another, I believed him. I believe it was mutual, too.'

I thought of Bill and myself. I had fallen in love with him at once, as he had fallen in love with me, so he claimed.

'She was an Italian princess, very wealthy, old world family. McKay at the time was penniless, just beginning his career, not a worthwhile credit to his name. Of course, her family would have none of it — told him to stay away, the works. But love, as you know if you've ever read any of McKay's novels, will find a way. The young couple eloped. She took the clothes on her back and a satchel full of diamonds that belonged rightfully to her. They came to America and married. As simple as that. Family railed, threatened, disowned her. It made no matter to the happy couple. They were in love, and life was their oyster.

'They made good use of those diamonds, too. Sold them one after the other, over the next several years, while McKay struggled along. They were gone before McKay's first big success. I know, because in the end he had to borrow heavily from friends. *Swan Song* sold just in time to save them from complete ruin. He was ten years paying off some of those debts. I know, because I managed his affairs for him by that time.

'So you see, my dear,' he said, coming closer, 'I know whereof I speak when I say that the diamonds are gone. If McKay made the remark the boy says he made — and it's even possible Jamie misunderstood — then it could only have been the fantasy wish of an old, dying man. Take my word for it, old men have their wishes too.'

I could barely suppress my disappointment. I had set great store, more than even I myself had realized, on what the attorney would be able to tell me. But, except for an interesting old story, he could tell me nothing.

No, I reminded myself, that was not true. He had in effect told me that I was mistaken in my fears. There was absolutely no motive for harming Jamie. I was certain he thought me a foolish young woman whose imagination had run away with her. In all fairness, I could hardly expect him to think of me any other way.

'Thank you,' I said, rising. 'I'm afraid I've put you to a great deal of bother for nothing.'

'It's never a bother to help a pretty young lady put her mind at rest,' he said gallantly, walking with me to the door. 'And more than that, I see that you are fond of the young boy, as I am. I appreciate your concern for him. By the by, the next time he comes into town, I hope he will come to see me.'

'I'm sure he will,' I said. 'Goodbye, and thank you again.'

'Not at all, my dear, and goodbye to you,' he said.

I walked dispiritedly in the direction of the hotel. I was almost there when a thought occurred to me, a thought so obvious that I actually laughed aloud at my own blindness and that of Amos Partridge.

The Christians believed the diamonds existed. Whether the gems were real or fantasy, so long as the Christians believed in them, they had their motive. How ironic, that the cause of the danger in which Jamie lived was as much a fool's end as the house in which the danger existed. The trail of fortune was only a blind path that led nowhere but to tragedy!

18

We left San Francisco that afternoon. Jamie was still filled with excitement over the trip, and he chattered incessantly of the things he and Bill had done together. I tried to share his buoyant mood, but I could not, and I soon lapsed into silence.

Bill began the trip home in high spirits, but he soon seemed to be infected by my lack of cheer, and before long he, too, had grown silent and withdrawn. I was grateful that Jamie seemed not to notice our moods.

Again and again I turned over in my mind the various possibilities open to me. If I could convince the Christians that there was no fortune hidden at Fool's End, nor anywhere else, it would probably remove the threat to Jamie's well-being. It was doubtful, however, that they would believe me if I were to convey the news to them. Even if I sent them to Mr. Partridge, they might easily suspect a collaboration to deceive them.

In the long run, would removal of the motive at this late date really make such a dramatic change? They were in blood stepped in so far, as it were, that to return would certainly be as dangerous as going on. Unless I was terribly mistaken, they had in some way engineered Anne's disappearance, they had made what I was certain were attempts on Jamie's life, and they had committed themselves to a criminal path. Would the discovery that their goal had been a hollow one deter them from that path? Or, more to that point, erase what they had already done?

If that was so, then my own pursuit was a fool's end as well. Had a treasure existed, I might have thwarted their efforts by finding it first and putting it safely elsewhere, but now I had nowhere to go.

'Looks like something's up,' Bill said aloud as we approached Fool's End. It was already evening. Jamie had finally succumbed to the weariness of excitement and was asleep in the back seat.

I looked toward Fool's End. The

outside lights were on, flooding the front of the house and the lawn with dramatic light. I would have expected this anyway, since we had called to say we were coming back; but in addition to this there were four cars parked in front, two of them highway patrol cars, the other two unfamiliar. A group of people stood clustered at the front steps.

I had an ominous presentiment, the feeling that someone had stepped upon my grave, and a chill went up and down my spine. I shivered and pulled my sweater close about my shoulders, but said nothing.

Bill seemed to have had the same premonition. As he pulled the car to a stop, he said, 'Maybe you'd better wait here and let me see what this is all about.'

'No,' I said, opening the door on my side. 'Better bring Jamie. I don't think you'll ever get him awake.'

I did wait, however, until Bill had taken Jamie from the back seat, carrying him in his arms; then we went together toward the steps. Grant was there, and Barbara, and several men, some of them in the uniforms of the highway patrol. They stood in silence, obviously waiting for us.

'Toby,' Grant greeted me, but he said nothing more.

One of the officers stepped forward. 'Miss Stewart?'

'Yes,' I said, waiting for him to offer an explanation.

'Sorry to bother you, miss, but we've had a little difficulty. I wonder if I could ask you to accompany us?'

'What's this about?' Bill asked.

'There's been an accident down the coast,' the officer explained, looking from Bill to me, and back to Bill again. 'Woman appears to have drowned.'

'Anne,' I said.

'Easy,' Bill said. He motioned to one of the patrolmen, who took Jamie. Then he put an arm about me to support me.

'We haven't identified the woman yet,' the officer explained. He looked genuinely distressed, and I found myself thinking how dreadful his job must be, to carry such unpleasant news to people. 'We've been trying to trace her, and the trail finally led us here. I understand your sister has been missing for some days?'

'Yes,' I said, leaning against Bill. My legs felt weak. 'She was here and she . . . she left.' I suddenly thought that I ought to have reported Anne as missing. Would it have made any difference? Would they even have believed me, if the Christians told a different story? Probably not.

'As I said, we don't know who this woman is,' the man went on. 'That's why we would like you to accompany us, to see if you can identify her. Understand, it may not be your sister; it could be just some poor girl from one of the towns up the coast.'

'I'll come,' I said.

'I'm coming with you,' Bill said. 'Let me put the boy to bed.'

The officer gave me a questioning look, perhaps wondering if I wanted Bill along. 'I'll help you get him settled in,' I said to Bill. We went past them and into the house, taking Jamie with us. He had half awakened, enough to question all the people.

'What's going on?' he asked sleepily.

'Nothing,' I told him calmly, tousling his hair. There would be enough unpleasantness this night without disturbing his young sleep.

He accepted my answer without question. Together Bill and I got him tucked neatly into bed. I hated leaving him, but I could scarcely take him with me on this trip.

'A few more minutes won't make any difference,' Bill said when we were back in the hall. 'Want some coffee?'

I shook my head. 'No, I'd as soon get it over with,' I told him.

We rejoined the people downstairs. Barbara had disappeared, presumably to go to bed. All but one of the cars had left, and all but two of the patrolmen. Grant still waited with them on the steps.

'Shall I come too?' Grant asked as we came down.

'Thank you,' I said gratefully, 'but I don't see what good that would do. Chances are it's only a false alarm anyway.'

The looks that the men exchanged told me they didn't believe that any more than

I did, but the remark was allowed to stand.

'You're probably right,' the officer in charge agreed.

We went in the patrol car, the two officers in front, Bill and I in the back. There was little conversation. Bill held my hand, and I was grateful for that silent communication, but I wanted nothing more at the moment. I knew that if I let myself lean on someone else now, I would lose all of the fragile strength that was supporting me. Once I surrendered to fear and despair, I would not again regain control.

Once on the highway the red lights were set flashing to clear the road, although there were in fact few cars out. We rode swiftly. I had an eerie sense of the night rushing past us beyond the delicate shell of the car. We hurtled through darkness, as shut off from the world beyond the closed windows as if we had been hurtling through space. We were alone in this capsule, the four of us.

Yet we were as cut off from one another

as we were the world outside. Our fragile links between one another were no stronger, perhaps less strong, then the link of radio communication that bound us to the headquarters from which the patrolmen worked. It was at least a constant sound, an unceasing muted conversation that bound hundreds of men together, making them one unit. We, for our part, had nothing to say.

It was nearly fifty miles to the town in question, at which the still unknown body had drifted ashore on a tide. It was late by this time, and the town folded up early. The streets were dark, only an occasional passing window winking its light at us in feeble welcome.

At the police station, however, there were many people, and many lights. I was aware that some of the people were reporters, but I gave them little attention. They watched us, sensing news. I thought of a trip once across the Southern California Desert, when my father had pointed out the giant, ghastly vultures hovering a little above the ground, watching some weakening creature that would soon be their life's blood.

We went past the main desk into a long hall. At the end of it a uniformed policeman sat at a little table. He rose as we approached. 'This the sister?' he asked the patrolman who had brought us. The officer nodded.

'I'd like to see the body first,' Bill said. They looked displeased that he should interfere with the normal procedure. 'I knew her sister,' he said.

'I can do it,' I said feebly. He gave my shoulder a squeeze.

'Stop trying to be a hero,' he said. 'Would you show me the body?' he said to the officers. He had such an air of authority that they seemed to surrender their arguments to him.

'In here,' the policeman said.

'Wait,' Bill said to me. Then they were gone.

I stood alone in the long, brightly lighted hall. They were gone for what seemed an eternity. Somewhere behind me I heard a clock strike. I could hear muted voices in another room. Everything seemed unreal to me. I thought any minute I would awaken from this grisly dream.

I had grown so accustomed to the aloneness that I started when the door swung open and Bill reappeared. He had paled visibly. He swallowed hard as he came out. I tried not to envision what he had seen.

His eyes met mine. He said nothing. There was no need. In his hand he held a tattered fragment of cloth. It was Anne's scarf; I recognized it at once.

For a moment I stood in frozen horror. Then, blessedly, darkness closed in around me, the darkness that had chased us along the highway.

★   ★   ★

The remainder of that night was a vague blur to me. I remember regaining consciousness in a clinical-looking room. A doctor was examining me.

The officers drove us back to Fool's End. I sat in the protective circle of Bill's arm. I did not let myself think. Not yet. I held back all of the thoughts that tried to

215

crowd into my dazed mind. There would be time for them in the morning. I would have many of them to face then. But not now.

At Fool's End Bill brushed by a still-waiting Grant and ushered me upstairs. Somehow Mrs. Haskins appeared to help me undress and get into bed. The rest was only a succession of nightmarish dreams in which my sister floated through murky waters, eyes staring but unseeing, skin as white as death.

It would have seemed that after the weeks of waiting, not knowing, gradually suspecting the truth, I should have been ready for the news of Anne's death. Certainly I had come to realize, even if I had not put the thought into concrete words, that there could be no other explanation for her continued absence. Yet the shock at having her death confirmed was an awful blow. Of course there was the sense of loss, the grief of being separated by death from one to whom I had always been so close.

Even more than that was the truth that

I had to face when I awakened the next morning and began to contemplate what had happened. Anne's death in a sense crystallized all of my fears regarding Fool's End. Before, I had dealt with intangibles, shadows that haunted the place, me, and Jamie; accidents that might not have been accidents; treasures that did not exist except in fantasy. Now I was faced with the ultimate reality: death.

I had been awake for a time when there was a tap at my door. Since I had awakened I had told myself that I did not want to face anyone. I had reveled in the sanctuary of the closed room, the safety of isolation. I wanted no one to disturb me. For a moment I did not answer the knock, silently wishing whoever was there to go away.

The tap came again, still soft. Suddenly I was done with being alone. In a flash I saw how wrong that was. There was no safety here, no comfort in shutting myself away. And even if there were, it was foolishness to want it. I had too much to do — for my own sake, for Jamie's sake, and most of all for Anne's sake. Whatever else I did or did not do, I meant to learn the truth about her death, and I would not accomplish that hiding in this big bed.

'Come in,' I called out, flinging back the bedcovers and grabbing my robe.

Jamie came timidly in. My angry voice must have frightened him. He paused warily inside the door. 'I heard about Anne,' he said. 'I'm sorry.'

A tear spilled out of my eye and ran down my cheek. I opened my arms to him and he came into them in a flash, flinging himself against me. We said nothing; it was not necessary to speak.

We were still in one another's arms when Bill knocked and, in response to my call, came in. 'Feeling a little better?' he asked.

'I'm all right,' I said.

'The Highway Patrol is downstairs,' he said. 'They want to talk to you. If you don't feel up to it, I can get rid of them.'

I blew my nose loudly. 'No, I'll be down in a few minutes. Ask them to wait. I'd like to talk to them too.'

He gave me a curious look, but he did

not question me. He nodded and went out to deliver my message. I sent Jamie on his way and dressed as quickly as I could.

Bill and Grant were both with the men in the den. I recognized one of the officers from the night before, but the other was a stranger. They were both polite and considerate, both expressing their regret at what had happened. They had brought my sister's effects with them in a small, neat bundle wrapped in brown paper. I took it, looking at it for a moment. It was all that remained of Anne. That bloated corpse from which the life had fled did not really count. It was not my sister, not anymore.

'Your sister drowned, of course,' one of the officers, the familiar one, said.

'You're quite sure of that?' I asked quietly.

They all looked at me then, Grant's head snapping around from looking out the window.

'Are you implying there might be some other cause of death?' the second patrolman asked.

I hesitated for a second. Dared I tell

them what I did think? If I meant to accuse the Christians, why not now? They could not harm me with these patrolmen here.

But what of later? And what of Jamie? And what, after all, could I tell them? I had no proof of my charges. The things that had happened were ostensibly accidents. I could tell them Anne had left without her clothing, and that her clothing had been destroyed when I discovered this — but the clothing was gone; there was no way to prove that charge. In the end, they would think me hysterical over the loss of my sister. They would leave, the Christians would send me away — and a helpless Jamie would be left behind.

'I was only asking,' I said aloud. 'When did she drown, do you think?'

'It's a little difficult to say for certain,' one of them explained. 'She was badly . . . she had been in the water some time. Maybe three weeks, even a little longer than that. At least two.'

She had died, then, immediately upon leaving Fool's End. If, that was, she had ever left Fool's End.

Had she fallen from the cliffs beyond this house? I could see them from the window at which Grant stood. Had she been thrown, perhaps unsuspecting?

'Are you all right?'

Bill was at my side. I realized that I had nearly fainted again. I shook my head weakly. 'Forgive me,' I said, standing with Bill's help.

The officers had stood also. 'We understand,' one of them said. 'There's not much we need for our report anyway. Probably the gentlemen can answer our questions.'

'I'm sure they can,' I said. 'Thank you,' I said to Bill, standing by myself. 'I'll be all right now. If you'll excuse me.'

Barbara came in as I was leaving. She paused to ask if I were feeling better, and to tell me how sorry she was. I was surprised at how moved she seemed. Her sympathy and sense of mourning were almost unreal. As if, I thought bitterly, she were acting. I thanked her and went on. I had nearly reached the stairs when I remembered that I had left the parcel with Anne's clothing in it behind in the den. I went back for it.

'She seems hysterical,' Barbara was saying as I came near. I paused; I had little doubt of whom she was speaking. 'It frightens me. You never know what people are going to do at times like these.'

I hesitated for a moment. Then I turned and retraced my steps. As I neared the stairs, Mrs. Haskins emerged from the dining room.

'I wonder, Mrs. Haskins,' I said when she had inquired after my health, 'If you would mind fetching a package that I left in the den. It's in brown paper.'

'Not at all, miss. Shall I bring it to your room?'

'Yes, please,' I said. I went on up.

She came into my room a short time later. In addition to the package, she had a tray of tea things. 'Miss Barbara thought you would want some fresh tea,' she said, setting things on the little table for me. 'She said it would make you feel better.'

'Thank you,' I said. 'And thank Mr. Christian also.'

When she had gone, I poured myself a

cup of the warm tea. It smelled delicious, and I was genuinely grateful for Barbara's show of thoughtfulness, even if it was only an act.

But an act for whom? I thought a moment later. Surely the policemen had gone by the time she ordered the tea. I went to the window and looked out. They were gone by now, although that proved nothing.

I went back to the tea and tasted it gingerly. Was it only my imagination, or did it have a bitter taste? Was I becoming paranoid, seeing ghosts in every corner? I heard the words she had spoken earlier: ' . . . You never know what people are going to do at times like these . . . '

Had she been preparing the stage for . . . for my suicide? It made sense, in a fiendish way. A hysterical girl — she had said that about me, too — grief-stricken by her sister's death. Her sister, her only living relative. And the parents had died just a short time before. If a girl like that were to take her own life, who would be surprised?

I carried the tea into my little bathroom

and poured it carefully down the drain, rinsing the cup and the pot well.

There would be no suicides for me, not if I had to eat grass. And there would be no falling from cliffs, and no getting pummeled by rocks. If anyone intended to do away with me, they would have to resort to less subtle means.

19

It was not until much later in the day that I decided to open the package that the patrolmen had brought. When I did, I felt a new wave of grief and nausea. Nearly rotted as they were, the tattered rags nonetheless brought back to me the memory of my sister — lovely, fresh, happy.

Of course they had no value, and no purpose but to renew grief. I decided to throw them away. As I put them into the wastebasket, however, something unusual caught my eye. There was a scrap of paper with them. I picked it out of the wastebasket. It was badly crumpled, but when I smoothed it out, the typing on it was still faintly legible. I took it to the light to study it more closely.

' . . . st men desire eternal salvation, women and food, in reverse order, it would . . . ' The rest of that line was torn away, and the other lines contained only one or two words. One contained four words: 'men and women really'. They made no particular sense, of course.

I went back to the long line. Most men, I thought it probably said, desire eternal salvation, women and food, in reverse order, it would seem. It read like something Walter McKay would say, although I did not recognize the quote. Probably it was one of the scraps from his personal papers such as I had been cataloguing, as Anne had before me.

Only, this was typed. McKay wrote in longhand, and normally did not type up his works until they were ready for a final draft. Anne must have typed this, and for some reason she had it with her when . . . when her accident occurred.

But why? Why this note, of all the notes? I read it again, looking for some particular significance, but I could find none. It was like a message from Anne, from beyond the grave, which I could not decipher.

I came down later. Bill was in the den, and I asked him if he would drive me into town.

'Of course,' he said. 'But are you sure it isn't something I could do for you?'

'No, this is something I have to do myself,' I assured him. 'There is one thing, though. The patrolman who was in charge last night. Do you happen to remember his name?'

He thought for a moment. 'Roberts, I think,' he said finally. 'Why?'

'I wanted to talk to him,' I said. 'I want to call him from town.' Then, thinking I ought to offer some sort of explanation, I said, 'It's just about my sister's things. A personal question.'

'You don't have to explain anything you don't want to,' he said simply.

* * *

I phoned from the drugstore in town, where there was a pay phone in a booth. Bill, perhaps through discretion, remained in the front of the store, where I could see him and see that he was not eavesdropping.

When I told my name, I was connected with the patrolman Roberts almost at

227

once. He again expressed his sympathy. He sounded pleasant and eager to be helpful.

'With my sister's things,' I said, 'I found a scrap of paper. I wasn't entirely certain that it ought to be there. Perhaps it got into the parcel by accident.'

'Oh no, ma'am,' he said without hesitation. 'I remember it because it was peculiar, actually.'

'Peculiar?'

'Well, it oughtn't have been there at all.' He was silent for a minute. When I made no reply, he tried to explain as politely as possible. 'The length of time in the water, you see; it should have rotted, or even floated away, or been eaten . . . sorry to have to say this . . . eaten by fish.'

'You needn't mince words,' I said. 'I'm quite all right now. I'm not at all hysterical.' I said it as calmly as I was able. I wanted to offset Barbara's hints.

'Anyway, this was clenched in your sister's fist so tight . . . well, I never saw anything quite like it. The nails had dug right into the flesh at the heel of the hand. It was like she was determined to protect it, to save it. Of course, that's probably fantasy. What probably happened was, she had it in her hand when she fell, and as she . . . when death set in, the muscles spasmed, trapping that little scrap there. When people drown, they seize things, seaweed and the like, and clench them that way. The only odd thing was that instead of grabbing out like a drowning person does, she held on to that paper.'

I thanked him and hung up. Bill was waiting patiently. 'Get it all straightened out?' he asked when I rejoined him.

I assured him I had. I did not offer any further explanations, and he did not ask any more questions. We rode back to Fool's End in silence.

The note haunted me. Had Anne, realizing that she would drown, saved that paper for some reason? Had she, through an effort of will, left me some clue to her death?

At the house, I went into McKay's office. I stared at the scraps upon which I had been working. Was I deluding myself in thinking the words on that note were McKay's? It was so little. Yet they sounded like his.

Or was I mistaken in thinking they had come from those miscellaneous scraps on which Anne and I had worked? Could they be instead from one of his books? Perhaps the clue was there, then, in the book, maybe even in the title.

I went to the case that contained all of his published works. My eyes went from title to title. I knew them all; I had read each of them at least once. But the phrase did not fit. I could not place it in any of the books. I read through the titles again, checking each of them off against my mental list. Still the connection would not come.

I went to the cabinets in which his papers were filed, opening a drawer at random. More notes waiting to be catalogued. I closed it and opened another. This one held the carbons of his published works. We had not bothered with these. Barbara had declared them of 'no value.' I had toyed with the idea of asking her if I might have them for sentimental reasons. I opened another drawer; still more carbons.

And that was when it came to me: the answer I had been seeking.

When I saw it, I saw it all at once, as if a curtain had been ripped aside to reveal the entire stage setting. It was so obvious, now that it was revealed to me, that I wondered that I had not seen it all before.

I began to look through the carbon copies. I thought I knew just where to look, and I was right. In a matter of seconds, I had found what the Christians had been seeking for weeks, maybe for months.

I had found *Liza's Diamonds*.

★ ★ ★

It was incredible. We had all of us searched for literal diamonds, when nothing could have been more logical than that Walter McKay had left a manuscript. I held it in my hands now, at least the carbon copy of the original. A manuscript entitled *Liza's Diamonds*.

Anne had found the original. Perhaps he had given it to her. She must have had it with her when she drowned, and had clung to that one scrap, literally deter-mined to leave a clue behind.

I took the manuscript to McKay's desk, turning on the light, and began to read. I could only skim it, turning the pages swiftly.

It was a memoir. It was a summing-up of his life, of his career, and of his attitude toward life. It was brilliant, witty, and wonderful. I found the scrap that Anne had clenched in her fist, and in context it assumed an altogether different meaning.

I read only enough to confirm that it was a new manuscript, and a fine one. McKay's last, and maybe his most important work. And it would, as he had prophesied, make Jamie wealthy. Any publisher would pay richly for this. It would be the publishing coup of the decade. It was literally worth a fortune.

It was a fortune that was rightfully Jamie's, but if the Christians learned of the existence of this manuscript, Jamie would never see a penny. If he even lived.

I knew what I had to do. First and foremost, this manuscript had to be saved. Even more than to Jamie, it belonged to the world, to posterity. Before anything else, I had to see that it was delivered into safe hands.

Working quickly, I packaged it for mailing. There was no time to write a letter, but that would not be necessary. I was certain that Amos Partridge would quickly realize what it was. I addressed it to the lawyer and sealed it.

I had once more to ask Bill to take me into town. I did not mind if he thought me foolish, or disorganized, or even crazy. If he thought any of these things, however, he kept them to himself and cheerfully insisted he did not mind.

I was torn by a desire to share my discovery with him. If I could only feel certain that he was an ally — but the risk was too great. Later, when I had made sure that both the manuscript and Jamie were safe, then I could beg his forgiveness, and see whether or not he still loved me. Until then I must turn a deaf ear to the clamoring of my heart.

I had brought the package in my carry-all so that it would not be seen. Bill waited outside the post office while I went in and mailed it, insured, to Amos Partridge. When that was done, I felt that a great weight had been lifted from my shoulders. I had done my duty to the world, and to Walter McKay.

And now, I thought, running down the steps to Bill's waiting car, I had to try to do my duty to McKay's grandson. I had already made up my mind to take Jamie away. I would do it that very night, under the cover of darkness.

'Everything all right now?' Bill asked as I got into the car again.

'Yes,' I assured him, managing a nervous smile. At least, I added mentally, it soon will be.

I did not know how much to risk telling Jamie. We had never discussed the things that had happened, although we seemed to understand one another without the need for lengthy explanations. I thought that it might be best to save the news of the manuscript until later, until we were safely away from Fool's End.

I went to him in his room. I had of course to tell him of my plans, and to trust to his discretion.

'I've got to ask you to do something,' I told him, 'and it will require that you trust me. Do you?' He nodded solemnly. 'I want to leave Fool's End tonight. And I want you to come with me.'

'You mean run away?' he asked.

'Yes. Without telling the others.'

He seemed to take it in his stride. If anything, the idea pleased him. I saw the gleam of adventure in his eyes. 'Where will we go?' he asked.

I had given a great deal of thought to that question, and had come up with only one answer. 'To your cousin in Los Angeles,' I said. 'Have you ever met him?'

'Once. He seemed like an okay guy.'

I hoped that he was. Certainly he was about to have a very tangled knot dropped on his lap. I had no plan but to tell him everything, and ask him to intervene for his young cousin's sake.

If that failed, then I would call in the police. This would no longer be a case of the local people being pacified by the Christians. There would be a kidnapping involved, maybe national publicity. By that time Amos Partridge would have the manuscript, and would perhaps have realized its significance. At the least, some sort of investigation would be launched, and the truth would ultimately be brought out.

That, at least, was what I hoped.

My plan was very simple. Bill left his keys in his car. I had done some driving, and if I was not particularly skilled, I was at least confident that I could get us away from here, to some place where we could catch a bus or a plane to Los Angeles. I meant to pack my things and Jamie's. Later, when the others had gone to bed, I would put them in the car. I had only to come for Jamie then, and we would leave. They would not discover our absence until morning. By then, we would be in Los Angeles.

I had not reckoned on Bill's using his car. So I was startled at dinner to hear him announce that he planned on driving into San Francisco during the night. 'I'll leave late,' he said, apparently to the table in general, 'and drive during the night. Get there fresh in the morning.'

I had difficulty eating the rest of my

dinner. If Bill went, he might be gone for days, during which we would have no way of escaping.

Although I wanted to run to my room immediately after dinner, I deliberately forced myself to linger, even having a second cup of coffee. Jamie customarily went up to his room immediately after dinner. I watched him go, knowing that he would not be going to his own room.

He was in mine when I came up. 'What are we going to do?' he asked in a whisper as soon as I came in.

'Leave,' I said. 'Now, before Bill does.' I had already packed most of my things and brought clothes for Jamie over to my closet, to pack them too. Now I took what was remaining and crammed it haphazardly into the cases. I had my own big case, and another that had been in the closet — a small one — plus my purse.

'Go to your own room and wait,' I told Jamie. 'If anyone comes, climb into bed and pull the covers up like you're asleep.'

When he had gone, I took the bags and made my way laboriously down the hall. It would have been simpler with his help, but I had discarded that idea. If I were discovered leaving with my bags, it would be one thing; if I were discovered with my bags and Jamie, it would be quite another.

I used the back stairs, praying that I would not encounter Mrs. Haskins. Luck seemed to be running in my favor. I made the back door without incident.

The garages were in a separate building. I half carried, half dragged the bags about the corner of the house. I reached the car. The keys were in it. I put the bags into the back seat and closed the door as quietly as I could. Then I began to run back to the house. We were as good as gone!

Jamie was waiting. He had heard me approach the door and, as I had instructed, climbed into bed, but when he saw me he threw back the covers and jumped out at once.

Then I heard steps on the stairs. I closed the door until it was open only a crack, through which I watched. Barbara came into view. My heart seemed to stop.

For a moment I thought she meant to

come into Jamie's room. There was no possibility of hiding before she came in. But she did not; she went on. She entered her own room, leaving the door open. After a moment she came out again, and returned downstairs.

When she was out of sight on the stairs, I took Jamie's hand and together we stole down the hall to the back stairs. As the door closed after us, I had an exhilarating sense of freedom. We had only to roll the car down the drive so that the sound of the engine would not alert the Christians, and we were on our way. Even with Bill's plans to leave tonight, we would have a good couple of hours before he discovered his car was missing; he had said he did not mean to leave until late.

We came about the corner of the house, and stopped. Bill stood not fifteen feet away from us, at his car. The car door was open, and he was examining our suitcases!

The luck that had seemed to smile on us had just abandoned us.

20

I moved back into the shadows, freezing motionless. If Bill came toward the house, he could not fail to see us. And he could hardly not grasp the significance of the cases he had found in the car. I looked about frantically. Escape to the main road was impossible without crossing the wide expanse of open lawn, where we would certainly be seen.

There seemed nothing for us to do but try to escape by the cliff path, but to flee that dangerous walkway in the darkness of night was as dangerous as to stay.

There was a sudden flash of light that spilled from the windows of one of the upstairs rooms, throwing a distorted outline across the lawn. I looked up. The light was from Jamie's window. A minute later, the lights of my room flashed on.

Our absence had been discovered! I looked down into Jamie's face. He was watching me with barely contained fear, and frightened as I was myself, I knew that for his sake I must summon the courage to get us out of the spot we were in.

I grabbed his hand in mine and we crept about the end of the house. When we were out of the range of Bill's vision, I whispered, 'Come on, we'll have to run for it.' We began to run toward the cliffs, up the incline. We had not quite reached the south corner when a finger of light splashed over the lawn off to our right, wavered, and then came tremblingly toward us. I seemed almost to feel it at our heels; then we were about the house, at the cliffs. Someone was in pursuit. The beam of the lantern caught us again; we dodged, eluding it.

I was breathless by the time we reached the path that led down the cliff and, partly from that and partly from the fear of descending this path in the dark, my legs felt weak and rubbery beneath me.

I hesitated for only a minute, holding Jamie back. 'Do you know it well enough to get us down it without a light?' I asked him.

He gave me a confident look; he seemed much less out of breath than I. 'I could run it with my eyes closed,' he assured me. 'Come on, I'll lead the way. Stay right behind me.'

I looked back once. The beam of a flashlight struck me full in the face. A voice — I couldn't be certain whether it was Grant's voice or Bill's, but only that it was a man's — cried, 'Stop right there!'

I did not stop. Jamie shot me a look and darted down the path. In an instant I was after him.

'I'll shoot!' the voice called, and this time I recognized it as Grant's voice. He couldn't shoot, though, because we were out of sight almost at once on the twisting path.

It was true, Jamie could run the path with the agility of a goat. Unfortunately, I could not. I had to hold to his hand and even so I kept tripping and stumbling. Once I cried aloud as my foot slipped and I might have fallen to the rocks below if Jamie hadn't been holding me.

A wave of despair broke over me. Grant knew the path as well as Jamie. At each bend in the path I could see the beam of his light getting closer. I knew in a moment he would catch up with us.

I let go Jamie's hand. 'You go ahead,' I told him. 'I'll keep Grant here long enough for you to get to the beach. Get help and come back.'

He came to a stubborn stop. 'I can't leave you here by yourself,' he said.

Of all the times for chivalry, I thought wryly — but there was no time to argue the point further. There was a scrambling of loose stones and dirt, and the light hit our feet, sweeping upward to our faces.

I faced him as sternly as I dared, shielding Jamie behind me.

'You little fool,' Grant said. Across the short space that separated us I could hear him breathing as heavily as I was.

'I can't see with that light in my face,' I told him, sounding far calmer than I felt.

My false confidence seemed to amuse him. He lowered the light, and when my eyes had readjusted to the night, I could see that he was smiling. 'Where did you think you were going?' he asked. I saw that in his other hand he carried a gun. I little doubted that he would use it if he felt compelled to. I had nothing but my wits with which to defend us, and right now they seemed to have abandoned me altogether.

'We were leaving,' I said bluntly. It would hardly have been worthwhile to pretend we were only out for a stroll.

'Why?'

I managed a hoarse laugh and gave my head a toss. 'I think we both know the answer to that.'

He smiled more broadly. 'Yes, I suppose we do,' he said. After a pause, he added, 'I have to admit, you have guts. I've always given you credit for that.'

'Unfortunately not enough brains, though, or I'd have left long before this,' I said.

His smile faded and he looked hard and cruel. 'I think perhaps we might go back now,' he said, indicating the direction from which we had come.

'Why,' I said, 'so that you can use that gun on us? If you mean to kill us, why not do it here and save us the walk back?'

'I'm not a murderer,' he said.

'No? What happened to my sister?'

'She fell. From this very cliff. Almost from this very spot, in fact.'

'I don't believe you,' I cried defiantly. I was certain he had killed Anne and that he meant to kill us as well; but I did not mean to kowtow to him, or to let him see me crying and begging.

'It's true,' he insisted. 'She tried to run away just as you did. I ran after her. I tried to tell her she'd break her neck, but she wouldn't listen. And she did just that. She tripped and went right over, into the ocean.'

I shuddered and closed my eyes to blot out the view. A gust of cold wind tugged at my skirt, seeming to draw me to the edge, only inches away. Beneath the narrow path where we stood I heard the sound of the waves lashing angrily at the rocks. I had a sudden vision of Anne, frightened, fleeing. I saw her stumble, saw her eyes widen with horror as she fell,

245

heard her anguished scream as she fell downward, downward . . .

I swayed dizzily and put a hand out suddenly to steady myself against the face of the cliff. It was damp and cold. I felt the harshness of a rock in contrast to the crumbling earth. The rock shook, exaggerating the trembling of my hand against its surface.

I had a sudden idea. I looked up at Grant Christian. He had been silent for a moment, studying me. 'You know,' he said thoughtfully, 'maybe we could work out a deal.'

'What kind of deal?' I asked. I inched forward, clinging to the cliff, until the loose rock was behind me, where he could not see as I worked it looser still with my fingers.

'I have no desire to harm you,' he said. 'All I care about is the diamonds. If you gave them to me, Mother would never have to know. I would let you go, and tell her you had taken them with you.'

'The diamonds?' I had forgotten that he still believed the diamonds were real.

He believed I had a fortune in gems with me. And now he was willing to bargain with me to get them.

Of course, I did not for a moment believe in his bargain. I had no doubt he would like the diamonds for himself, with no one else knowing he had gotten them, but there wasn't the vaguest possibility of his letting Jamie and me escape to tell anyone else of the diamonds, of all that had happened, of Anne's death, of the attempts on our lives. No, he wanted to get the diamonds he thought I possessed, without risk of my falling into the ocean with them.

I did not say all of these things as they flashed through my mind. I had my fingers almost about the rock at my side, it was nearly free of the earth that had held it perhaps for centuries. In another moment I would pull it loose.

'I haven't any diamonds,' I told him, hoping for a few more seconds of time.

He snarled angrily and gestured threateningly with the gun. 'Don't give me any of that,' he snapped. 'Do you take me for a fool? I'm giving you a chance to save your life, because I was raised as a gentleman. But I warn you, if you force me, I'll take them from you.'

'And if I do give them to you?' I asked.

'I told you,' he said in a gentler tone of voice. 'I'll let you go right on down the path, and I'll go back and say you escaped with the jewels.'

'Both of us?'

'Of course, both of you,' he said impatiently.

My fingers were raw and bleeding. I tugged, but the rock remained stubbornly imbedded in the side of the cliff. 'Tell me one thing,' I said, still working for time. 'Was Bill a part of your machinations?'

'Bill? Hah. He's too damned pure and innocent all of a sudden. It's not as if he hasn't ever done anything wrong in his life — Las Vegas, liquor, a string of girls that would stretch from here to Buenos Aires. And what have we got from him for weeks? Lectures on the brat's welfare, warnings not to try anything tricky, a lot of snoopy questions about your sister's disappearance. Don't worry, I'll see that he gets his due when the time comes.' He spoke with bitter vehemence, but his words made my heart sing. Bill was not one of them. Even in my perilous situation I could not resist a smile.

He saw the smile and misinterpreted it as meaning his suggestion pleased me. 'Yes, it makes more sense doing it my way, doesn't it? Look, maybe we could even work out something a little better. If the diamonds are even half what I expect, there's plenty for both of us.'

The earth gave about the rock and it came into my hand. Grant took a step toward me. His cruel, hard face had assumed a flirtatious look.

There was a sudden scrambling sound from above. I gasped aloud as Bill's voice called, 'Toby!'

Grant swore under his breath. A short distance behind him the path curved about the face of the cliff. A rock clattered into view, warning of Bill's approach.

'Bill,' I cried aloud, 'he has a gun!'

Bill swung into view, his face angry, and stopped. Grant swung about and raised the gun to fire.

I threw the rock. It struck Grant lightly, just grazing the side of his head. However, it was enough to throw him off balance. He fired, but the shot went wildly upward, missing Bill.

Grant swayed, trying to regain his footing on the precarious path. He stepped to the side and brought his foot down on nothing but air.

Bill grabbed for him, but it was too late. While Jamie and I watched, transfixed with horror, Grant toppled over the edge. A terrible scream tore the night air as he fell. Then it ended, and there was only the pounding of the waves below, and our own labored breathing.

Bill and I stared at one another across the space that separated us. 'Well,' he said gently, 'are you going to run from me, too?'

'No,' I sobbed, coming into his waiting arms. 'Not any longer.'

We met Barbara on the path. Grant's scream had brought her from the house. The anger with which she initially greeted us quickly turned to fear.

'It's no use,' Bill told her crisply.

'Grant's gone. And he said and did enough before he went to spoil the whole business for you.'

She looked suddenly defeated and old. I did not get an impression that she was mourning her son. She looked merely like a bad loser.

'Tell me,' she said, looking me coldly in the eye, 'did you find the diamonds?'

My laugh was enough to make her angry again.

When we had come back into the house and Bill had sent Mrs. Haskins to ask the neighbors to summon the police, we had time for explanations. I explained about the manuscript and what I had done with it. I admitted also where Jamie and I had been going, and why.

'I'm truly sorry,' I said to Bill, 'that I couldn't turn to you. But I just couldn't know how much you were involved.'

'It's all right,' he said, squeezing my hand. 'You had reason to be frightened. It might have helped if I had been more frank, but I didn't want to frighten you with my suspicions regarding your sister. I knew something was fishy around here;

that Grant and Barbara were looking for something at night when they thought I'd never see them. Then when Anne suddenly disappeared, I really got worried. I even stole her letter from your room to see if it had any clues you hadn't caught on to.'

'I knew it was you who had taken that,' I admitted with a rueful smile. 'That was one of the things that made me unsure of you.'

'And that accident must have made it look worse,' he added. He took me in his arms. 'But that's all behind us now.'

Jamie had been dozing, trying to listen but not quite able to remain alert. He suddenly sat upright and asked a question that must have been bothering him for some time. 'What's going to happen to me?'

It gave my heart a pang to think of him as an orphan. But Bill, apparently, had already considered that question. 'I think I know a couple who'll take you in,' he said. 'Newlyweds. Or at least they soon will be.'

I did not fully understand his remark

until he looked at me again and said, 'By the way, we'll have to go back to San Francisco pretty soon. There's a fur in storage there that rightfully belongs to you.'

THE END

We do hope that you have enjoyed reading this large print book.

Did you know that all of our titles are available for purchase?

We publish a wide range of high quality large print books including:
Romances, Mysteries, Classics
General Fiction
Non Fiction and Westerns

Special interest titles available in large print are:
The Little Oxford Dictionary
Music Book, Song Book
Hymn Book, Service Book

Also available from us courtesy of Oxford University Press:
Young Readers' Dictionary
(large print edition)
Young Readers' Thesaurus
(large print edition)

For further information or a free brochure, please contact us at:
Ulverscroft Large Print Books Ltd.,
The Green, Bradgate Road, Anstey,
Leicester, LE7 7FU, England.
Tel: (00 44) 0116 236 4325
Fax: (00 44) 0116 234 0205

ROOKIE COP

Richard A. Lupoff

America, June 1940. Nick Train has given up his dreams of a boxing championship after a brief and unsuccessful career in the ring. When one of his pals takes the examination for the police academy, Nick decides to join him. But what started out as a whim turns into a dangerous challenge, as Nick plays a precarious double game of collector for the mob and mole for a shadowy enforcement body . . . Will the rookie cop's luck hold?

THE DEVIL'S DANCE

V. J. Banis

When Chris leaves New York for a vacation with her half-sister Pam, who is staying at a Tennessee country mansion, she discovers that the remote backwater is the site of a centuries-old feud raging between the Andrewses and the Melungeons; and Chris's elderly host, Mrs. Andrews, lives in fear. Danger lurks everywhere, from the deceptively tranquil countryside to the darkly handsome, yet mysterious, Gabe who hides amid the shadows. And when events take a more sinister turn, it seems that the curse of the Melungeons is hungry for more victims . . .

FIND THE LADY

Norman Firth

When gangster Mike Spagliotti is found shot through the head inside his locked New York hotel suite, it is a perplexing problem for Detective-Inspector Flannel. And when newspaper reporter Anita Curzon begins to interfere, Flannel's temper does not improve . . . In *The Egyptian Tomb* Tony Gilmour and his friends Ron and Alan travel to Egypt to investigate the suspicious death of Ron's father — but they are dogged by enemies who will stop at nothing to ensure that no one discovers the secret of the tomb of Ko Len Tep!